WELCOME TO THE HOUSE OF BRASS

With sightless eyes, the ancient, wizened man stared at the six men and women in his vast living room.

In a cackling voice, he told them they had been summoned out of gratitude to their late parents, all of whom had given Brass vital aid in the shifting course of his long life. In return, the millionaire wanted to select the best among those present to be his heirs.

There was but one detail wrong with this explanation. The parents in question had been Hendrik Brass's most vicious enemies.

And their descendents had been summoned not out of gratitude, but out of obsessive hate . . .

"A dandy Queen brain-teaser . . . it's even better than its predecessors"
—Des Moines Tribune

THE HOUSE OF BRASS

Ellery Queen

A SIGNET BOOK

Published by The New American Library

Library of Congress Catalog Card Number: 68-13406

This is a reprint of a hardcover edition published by The New American Library, Inc. The hardcover edition was published simultaneously in Canada by General Publishing Company, Ltd.

SIGNET TRADEMARK REG. U.S. PAT. OFF. AND FOREIGN COUNTRIES
REGISTERED TRADEMARK—MARCA REGISTRADA
HECHO EN CHICAGO, U.S.A.

SIGNET BOOKS are published by
The New American Library, Inc.,
1301 Avenue of the Americas, New York, New York 10019

First Printing, April, 1969

PRINTED IN THE UNITED STATES OF AMERICA

. . . for within the hollow crown
That rounds the mortal temples of
  a king
Keeps Death his court, and there
  the antic sits,
Scoffing his state and grinning at
  his pomp;
Allowing him a breath, a little
  scene,
To monarchize, be fear'd, and kill
  with looks,
Infusing him with self and vain
  conceit
As if this flesh which walls about
  our life
Were brass impregnable . . .

—SHAKESPEARE,
King Richard II, III, ii.

BRASS— / bras, bräs / *n* [ME *bras, OE braes;* c. OFris *bres* copper, MLG *bras* metal] **1:** any of various metal alloys consisting mainly of copper and zinc **2:** a utensil, ornament, or other article made of such an alloy **3:** *Mach.* a replaceable semicylindrical shell, usually of bronze, used with another such to line a bearing; a half bushing **4:** *Music.* **a.** a musical instrument of the trumpet or horn family **b.** such instruments collectively or in a band or orchestra **5:** *Brit.* **a.** a memorial tablet or plaque incised with an effigy, coat of arms, or the like **b.** *Slang.* money **c.** *Slang.* a prostitute **6:** *Furniture.* any piece of ornamental or functional hardware, as a drawer pull, made of brass **7:** metallic yellow; lemon, amber, or reddish yellow **8:** *U.S. Slang.* **a.** high-ranking military officers **b.** any very important officials **9:** *Informal.* excessive assurance; impudence; effrontery—*adj* **10:** of, made of, or pertaining to brass **11:** using musical instruments made of brass **12:** having the color brass—**brass'ish** *adj.*

Chapters

1

WHAT?

Richard was all for San Juan or St. Croix, but Jessie held out for every girl's right to one honeymoon in Niagara Falls (she said "girl" bravely, taking advantage of the technicality); so Niagara Falls it turned out to be, Richard giving in without a fight. He was so much in love he would have agreed to Hanoi.

Ellery received his father's cable in an Istanbul hotel room and collapsed on the bed. He was on a planetary junket, nibbling at police chiefs for gourmet crimes, and he had encountered no criminological recipe so outré as the Inspector's announcement. His first thought was of old fools; but when he flew to New York he found Jessie Sherwood to be, not an old man's nubile folly, but a brisk and buxom dear approaching fifty, with a young voice and young eyes, full of soft humor and authority, and without duplicity or doubts. They scouted the opposition for a moment, decided there was none, and fell into each other's arms.

The couple were married in Jessie's little church in the Village, and afterward Ellery gave them a reception at the Algonquin, out of an obscure sentiment toward the memory of Frank Case and the Round Table, in a suiteful of spring flowers. Jessie wore an Irish lace dress the color of blue violets, like her eyes, and the Inspector a summer tuxedo (peevishly vetoing Ellery's overenthusiastic suggestion of a cummerbund), and Ellery had the unique experience of giving his father away. The minister out of the quaintness of his Episcopal heart spoke of the blessings of matrimony "in the summer of our content," which Jessie thought a beautiful way of putting it, while her groom glared at the man of God, who was a good twenty years younger than he and could afford to be patronizing.

The continuation of the beginning was very, very satisfactory. The mighty Falls roared an unending welcome and offered them its shiniest sunlight, rainbow, and mist. And the fat Indian woman squatting near the railing sold them pillows stuffed with pine needles that scented their double bed with sanctification.

When they got back from the honeymoon, looking well-fed, they went to the Queen apartment. Jessie had given hers up, putting her things in storage against the undiscussed future. It kept seeming as if there would always be time enough to talk about it.

"Home." Jessie crooned over the word. Then she clucked over the dust and began bustling about opening windows.

The old man dumped their bags. "Is it?"

Why, Richard, whatever do you mean?"

"What are we going to do about Ellery?" So it came out.

"Oh, pooh," Jessie said. "I made up my mind long ago. Ellery will live with us, and that's that." She went hunting for a dustcloth.

"Maybe he will," the Inspector mumbled, "and then again maybe he'll have something to say about it. He usually does." And he began thumbing through the accumulation of mail he had found waiting for him. "We'll see."

"We won't see," Jessie said, reappearing. "You haven't lost a son, you've gained a wife."

"It's beginning to sink in," the Inspector said with a grin. "All right, let's say it's settled for the time being."

"Why does it have to be temporary? Where would we get an apartment these days we could afford? Even with me working—"

"With you what?" the retired Inspector cried.

"Working."

"You're not going back to nursing! I want a wife, not a proctologist's plumber. My police pension'll be enough, along with what I've stashed away. I didn't marry you to watch you carry bedpans for a lot of neurotic women—or *men!*—and don't you forget it, Jessie Queen."

"Yes, Richard," Jessie said meekly. But she thought: I will. We'll need the money. "What's wrong?"

He was glaring at one of the envelopes. "This is addressed to Miss Jessie Sherwood. Your first letter, and they don't pay me the courtesy of using my name!"

"Forwarded by Registry. It's probably some charity asking for money. I'm on all sorts of lists."

It was not a plea for money. Jessie looked, and frowned, and looked again. "I'll be darned."

"What is it, Jessie"

"Look at this."

This turned out to be a $100 bill.

"And that."

And that was half a $1000 bill.

The Inspector frowned at the pretty portraits, too. Experience had taught him that mysteries starting out with unsolicited lucre had a way of turning nasty toward the end, if not sooner. For fillip, the original of the $1000 bill had been scissored down the middle of Grover Cleveland's bust with a pinking shears in three op-art-looking jags.

"Richard, whatever can it mean?"

He was holding the bills up to the light off the end of his nose. "They're not counterfeits. How should I know? There's got to be some explanation. Look in the envelope, Jessie. There must be a note."

There was, and they touched heads bending over it. Unfolded, it became two sheets of vellum notepaper bearing a heavily engraved gold crest, all very impressive; or it would have been impressive if it had not had the foxed look of paper that has been lying around for a generation. The body of the letter was typewritten, as was the address on the envelope.

"Out of somebody's attic, looks like. Read it aloud, Jessie." The Inspector's reading glasses were over near the old leather chair. "Damn my eyes!" He regularly damned each part of his anatomy that surrendered to his years; this year it was his eyes.

Jessie's soft voice gave the contents of the note a femininity that rather got in the way of its style. "'Dear Miss Sherwood,'" the foxed vellum said. "'You will doubtless think it odd to receive an invitation from someone you do not know. I give you my word, however, that this is all very much to your interest.

"'I invite you herewith to visit me at The House of Brass, my ancestral home near Phillipskill, New York.

"'The $100 bill enclosed will serve to cover your traveling expenses. As for the missing half of the $1000 bill, it will be presented to you at the expiration of your visit. Call it a souvenir of what I think I may assure you will be an unusual experience.

"'Taxis are available at either the Tarrytown or Phillipskill railroad stations, although Phillipskill is somewhat nearer. If you should decide to come by motor, take the second turn on your left after passing the Old River Inn on the Albany Post Road; then the first turn to the right, which is marked by a sign that says Private Road. As for water transportation, the old boat landing has been in disrepair for many years, and I cannot vouch for its safety.

"'May I hope to expect you as soon as possible. Your arrival or absence will reply for you. In the latter case, of course, the halved $1000 bill will be of no use to you. In any case, you may retain the $100 bill.

Yours faithfully,
Hendrik Brass' "

The signature was old-man shaky, Jessie observed—an old-fashioned old man, she thought, from the language. She remarked this to Richard, who went for his glasses to see for himself.

"An old boy, all right. And of the old school. I take it you don't know a Hendrik Brass?"

"Never heard of him."

The Inspector reached for the telephone. "Velie'?" he said to the Sergeant when the familiar basso blasted his ear. "Sure I'm back! Fine, she's fine. Listen, Velie—yes, I'll tell her. Remember that Fifth Avenue place called The House of Brass? What became of it. How about a man named Hendrik Brass?—Hendrik, ending in *ik*. You're a fat lot of help. Sure, first chance we get." He hung up. Jessie looked at him anxiously.

"The House of Brass used to be a high-toned jewelry store on Fifth Avenue, like Tiffany's and Cartier's. You had to have real moola to walk in there, Jessie. As I recall the place, it specialized in gold—solid gold services, that sort of stuff. They closed the shop years ago. Velie says they never reopened. Not in New York, anyway."

"But the letter talks about The House of Brass as if it's a place to live in, Richard."

"Doesn't he call it the ancestral home? I guess he just uses the old firm name for it."

Jessie's little nose twitched like a rabbit's. "I swear, Richard, I don't know what to do about this."

"I know what I'd do."

"What?"

"Send the money back and forget it."

"Would you really?" In spite of herself, Jessie felt a lick of disappointment. Her life had been a succession of stuck movie frames—night duty, whining women, unsavory bedpans, men patients who either pinched your bottom or looked as if they would like to, and the eternal triangle of nurse, intern, and supervisor. What her life had lacked was the unexpected, and here it was being offered her on a silver platter, or rather in a gold-crested letter. And Richard, dear new husband, was saying to send the bright bills back and forget the whole thing. "Oh, Richard," Jessie heard herself say in a rush, "let me!"

He was wonderful. He looked at her with his bushy-browed stare; then the whole hard face melted and ran, and he took her in his arms. "How could I ever deny you anything, honey? But my advice is to get more information. How about giving this Hendrik Brass a ring and finding out first if he's got all his marbles? You can sometimes tell just from the way they sound. I'll call for you if you want."

"Would you, darling?"

"You bet," he said; and jumped for the phone.

But Westchester Information had no listing for a House of Brass or a Hendrik Brass, and he set the phone down with a scowl. "If not for the cash, I'd say it was a practical joke. Jessie, I don't *want* to deny you, but . . ."

Men had to be male, especially new husbands; Jessie was not alarmed. Instead, she kissed him. "I'm eaten up by plain nosiness, darling. Don't tell me you aren't."

"If you think I'd let you go traipsing off by yourself—"

"I wouldn't dream of it. Oh, Richard, this sounds like an adventure! What a thrilling way to start our married life."

How right she was.

"DeWitt Alistair" sounded like a made-up name in a third-rate play played by a fourth-rate company. But it happened to be Alistair's legal monicker, which he used only when the mark needed a particular kind of softening up. As it had turned out, he would have been better advised to use something that sounded as if it came out of *Pilgrim's Progress,* like John Repentance or Reuben Disappointment.

To make matters grittier, Mrs. Alistair, who had had her doubts from the beginning, kept throwing the biter-bit bit in his teeth. She managed this feat without opening her mouth, an accomplishment that few appreciated but her husband, who had long since given up admiring it.

So the Alistairs were not in connubial harmony when they entered the lobby of the shabby-genteel hotel in the West 60s that Alistair had insisted reflected their working image and that, it now appeared with bitter clarity, their true image could not afford. The fish had taken their bait, slipped the hook, and vanished downstream, leaving them hungry and furious. The immediate problem was to find a less knowledgeable trout, and the wherewithal to land him. They paid only perfunctory attention to the impressive-looking envelope in their box. Impressive-looking envelopes did not impress them. They had mailed too many of them.

Both were thinking deeply.

Upstairs, in their shabby-genteel room, Alistair tossed the envelope on the bed, sat down near the dusty window, and turned to the racing news in the paper he had picked up from a lobby chair. Mrs. Alistair unlocked one of their two suitcases. From it she took an electric plate, a whistling teakettle minus the whistle, a spoon, two plastic cups, and a nearly empty jar of instant coffee. She filled the kettle at the tap in the bathroom, placed it on the hot plate, plugged the plate in at the outlet behind her husband's chair, and returned to the bathroom to repair her face, which was aristocratic-plain, well-preserved, noncommittal, and served her purposes. When she came out she planted herself before her spouse and looked at him. After a moment he lowered the paper.

"Well, what are you looking at?" DeWitt Alistair had a thunky voice, with a British edge to it that gave off a faint thud of counterfeit. It was. He had been born in Weehawken, New Jersey.

"Well," Elizabeth Alistair replied, "not very much." Her speech was entirely unaffected. What there was of it.

"There you go again!"

"Haven't said a word."

"Haven't you!"

"Quote me."

"I'll clip you!"

His wife seemed undaunted. "What do we do now, Machiavelli?"

"I've got to think about it," he said shortly.

"You won't find the answer in the harness entries."

"Let me alone, will you!"

"Any money left?"

He returned to his newspaper, shrugging.

Mrs. Alistair spooned out the coffee, added the water, stirred, and set one of the cups down at his elbow. Then she did the same for herself. All in an exhausted way. It was one of their longest dialogues in months.

She sat down on the bed and sipped her brew, giving herself completely over to thought. The process was evidently not agreeable; it foretold disaster for someone.

Suddenly she picked up the letter and opened it.

Alistair grunted something unpleasant to himself and turned the page. He looked like Walter Pidgeon, but with mean little eyes like a *corrida* bull. He was not a good man to meet in an alley. Or to play cards with.

"DeWitt."

"What now, for God's sake?" He glanced over. She was holding up a mint $100 bill and what looked remarkably like half a mint $1000 bill. He extended his hand quickly. She gave him two sheets of rusty-looking vellum notepaper. The bills she retained.

"I'll take the whole one," he said. "You can keep the half."

Mrs. Alistair smiled at his transparency. She handed over the $100 bill and tucked the mutilated bill away in her cleavage. Alistair held the $100 bill up to the light. Then, without comment, he placed it in his wafer wallet and turned to the letter. When he had finished reading the letter he stored it carefully in his breast pocket.

"What do you think, Liz?"

"Come-on."

"I'm not so sure."

"That's an improvement," she said, and rose.

"Nothing to lose. And there's the other half of the grand."

"Pigeon bait," she said reflectively.

"What can he get out of us? So we bite. Agreed?"

She shrugged.

Alistair picked up the telephone, said, "Time, please," listened, and hung up. "Twelve minutes to checkout," he said to his wife, and rose, too.

Elizabeth Alistair washed the cups and spoon and dried them on a hand towel, deposited them in the smaller suitcase along with the jar of coffee and the hot plate, and locked the case. Her husband put on his Tyrolean hat and charcoal-gray Wales of Boston weatherproof, and picked up the larger of the two cases. His wife went to the closet and got out her Russian lynx coat, a memento of a bygone bonanza which she kept in rack-new condition. She tucked the beige velvet toque carefully on her dyed hair, looked around, picked up the smaller case and, as an afterthought, her husband's stolen newspaper, and preceded him from the room.

Neither looked back.

It was indicative of Dr. Hubert Thornton's quality that the patients of the South Cornwall Medical Group called him "Doc," while they addressed his three medical partners as "Doctor." To the partners this was symptomatic of his weakness, and they were forever chiding him about it. "All right, so you're a kindly old g.p.," the heart and lungs man of the Group jeered. "But do you have to lay it on so thick, Hube? It makes the rest of us look like medical sharks."

"I don't try to," Hube Thornton protested. "It just comes out that way."

"Take the Andersons' bill. It's been deliquent for seven months. What's so great about the Andersons? You sleeping with Mrs. Anderson or something?"

Thornton flushed. "Mrs. Anderson has a prolapsed uterus and a peptic ulcer," he said stiffly.

"Neither stopped her from buying two cases of bourbon and Scotch for that wingding they threw last Saturday night. If the dame can buy booze in case lots she can damn well pay her medical bill. The trouble with you, Hube, is you're trying to be South Cornwall's Albert Schweitzer. Who's going to pay our bills?"

"You're right, of course." And Thornton took out his fat old Waterman pen and wrote the Medical Group his personal check for the amount of the Andersons' bill.

It made for an embarrassed silence.

"That ties it," said the pediatrician of the Group with a snap of his jaws on the cigar in his mouth. "You have a genius for making me feel like a son of a bitch, Hube. You can take your check and shove it." He tore it up. "All right, men, we wait some more. Hube Thornton Rides Again."

The tall surgeon of the Group shook his Ivy-League-barbered head. "Hube, you should have gone into the Public Health Service. You spend more time in that clinic and make more night calls than the rest of us put together."

"Somebody has to," Dr. Thornton said feebly.

"You were born in the wrong century. You know you've got bags under your eyes an inch thick? Ozzie here insists you're an incipient TB. And why the hell don't you get your glasses fixed? You look like a Skid Row bum. And buy another suit?"

They ran through a long list of chronic grievances.

Thornton remained silent. He had tried more than once to withdraw from the Group for the sake of the common weal; to his bewilderment they always jumped on him as if he had proposed that they start performing illegal abortions.

He was forty-seven years old, scalpel-thin, with hair turning to cancer gray and a high-temperature mustache that was too much trouble to keep trimmed—hell, he thought with a chuckle, if it doesn't make me look like Dr. Schweitzer at that! Food meant nothing to him, although a brandy once a night, before bedtime, usually did. The eyeglasses charge was also justified: a shaft had snapped months before and he had mended it with adhesive; he had simply never found the time to have a new shaft fitted. As for the sartorial lapse, you always had to have a suit pressed or a Merthiolate spot removed, or waste good time buying a new one.

After a while Hube Thornton stuffed his hairy ears to the three-man recitation of his vices and virtues—virtues that always seemed, in their view, to be vices in themselves—and thought of other things. He was brought back to time and place by a sharp pronunciation of his name.

"What?" Thornton said.

"I said," the pediatrician said, "that girl out there with the hairdo is one continuous pain in the gluteus. Put a letter addressed to you in my mail. Third time this week." He tossed a heavy envelope over. "Maybe it's someone paying a bill, God forbid."

His partners suddenly began to talk golf, lying their heads off. Dr. Thornton opened the envelope. He took out what was in it and gargled.

"Good God!" the heart-and-lungs man exclaimed. "It's money! Hube's caught himself an honest patient."

"Honest my foot," the pediatrician cried. "He's loaded. Say, isn't that thousand dollar bill cut in half?"

"At least the hundred's whole," the surgeon said. "But who pays in cash these days?"

"Where?" Thornton paused in his reading. "I mean, where is Phillipskill?"

"Near Tarrytown," said the h.-and-l. man. "House call? With that kind of fee, I'd make it myself."

"I'll be jiggered." Thornton wagged his big head. "Will you for heaven's sake read this?"

The two sheets of vellum were passed around. There were appropriate comments from his colleagues.

"But you can't get away from this money," Thornton said. "They certainly look genuine. Do you suppose he's psycho?"

The three modern doctors exchanged glances. The surgeon nominated himself spokesman.

"Hube," he said earnestly, "here's your chance."

"Chance for what?"

"To get off the treadmill. Why not take the guy up on this? He's probably an oddball millionaire who was on the right side in the Medicare fight. How about it, Hube? Hell, it'll be a ball."

"Besides," said the pediatrician, "you can use a vacation."

"And how," said the heart-lungs man. "Or one of these days, by God, I'll find your sputum full of mycobacterium bugs, and then you'll get a vacation that'll cost you."

"But I can't just go off! What about my practice?"

"We'll get Joe Adelson to fill in—he's full of the milk, too," said the surgeon. "And if there's still some slack, Hube, we'll take it up. Go on, for once in your life act human. What have you got to lose but your bags?"

"My clinic patients—"

"We'll handle them, too."

It took them thirty-five minutes by the office clock to talk Hube Thornton into responding affirmatively to the mysterious Mr. Brass's summons. By that time the outer office was jammed with the usual early-morning prothrombins, low-grade upper respiratory infections, and emergency hangovers, and Hube said all right, but only if they let him clear his appointments calendar for the day, even if it took him, Schweitzer-wise, far into the night.

Miss Openshaw found the squarish envelope in her letter box in the vestibule, mixed in with the usual pleading letters from the Institute for the Indigent Blind, the Ocapoosa Indian Mission School, the Leper Hostel, and other desperate institutions of good works, and set about climbing the two flights of the brownstone to her maidenly apartment.

En route she had to brave the morning ordeal, which consisted in passing Mr. Bailey's apartment door. The man was appalling, with all too obvious designs on every female spoor whose path he crossed. It made her blood run cold to see that mysterious door open a crack and the evil brown eye leer out at her.

Sometimes he opened his door to the fullest, so that she could see him in all his male vulgarity. He had a coarse way of not buttoning his shirt, exposing the ugly hair on his chest. Once he had actually dared to accost her. Oh, he had been clever. An innocent-sounding "Good morning, neighbor." It was the only time she had ever heard his voice, which was deep and gruff and—oh, what word was there but *male*!—and she had heard herself with absolute stupefaction asking him up to her apartment for tea. To her apartment! What under Heaven had come over her? By a miracle she had gone unscathed. Actually, the man had refused. She could picture, only too graphically what would have happened had he accepted her inane invitation. It had been a narrow escape.

Miss Openshaw's step slowed as she approached the Bailey door on the landing this morning and, inevitably, passed it. That was strange, because her heart was bumping and her mind was telling her that she must hurry before that door opened and he revealed himself in all his disgusting hairiness; but somehow her limbs would not obey her.

Fortunately, nothing happened. His door remained closed, and Miss Openshaw went on up the other flight to her door, clutching the mail and her fears to her bosom.

Cornelia Openshaw was thirty-nine and, as the saying went, "never kissed"—at least since childhood, and even then only sparingly by her mother, who had favored boys, and never by a father who was as remote as Jehovah. She gave the impression of being not so much plain as unused. Ordinarily she was mouse-mannered, but there were times when she seemed touched by a live wire; at such times she appeared about to leap. She was always heavily made up; she spent hours at her vanity, which was crowded with choice items from Helena Rubinstein's cosmetic counters. She invariably made her toilette before her morning descent to the mailbox and the dangerous crossing of the first-floor landing.

She hurried into her apartment, locked her three locks, slipped the guard-chain into its slot, and ran over to pull down a windowshade that showed four inches of daylight. She had a horror of Peeping Toms, although of late she had noticed with some perturbation that she was becoming forgetful about the shades.

She sat down on her Regency sofa to go through the mail. The tea she had poured before going downstairs was cold, and she rose to heat it; there was no urgency about the mail; she never received any of importance except the modest estate checks on which she lived. When the tea was hot, she reseated herself and, sipping daintily, reached for the first envelope.

It was heavy and squarish.

The elegance of the vellum warmed her. One rarely saw notepaper of such quality in these days of mass cheapness. Whom could it be from?

When the money fell out she gasped.

She read the letter avidly.

Its contents immediately suffused her. Who was Hendrik Brass? It sounded like a foreign name, and Cornelia Openshaw did not like foreign names. Beware the Greeks bearing gifts. . . . Gifts. Of course! It was the beckoning candy to the innocent child, with who knew what at the giving end. His courtly style might be a lure. After all, he was inviting her to come to a place that was very likely, from the sound of it, miles from a police station—probably in a wooded area, where her body might not be found for years, after his will had been done on her. Miss Openshaw was an indefatigable reader of true crimes, books like *The Boston Strangler* and *In Cold Blood,* shuddering at every detail and trying to imagine the unimaginable others.

The sensible thing to do was to take the letter and money straight to the police.

She reached for the telephone.

But something drew her back—curiosity, or a dollop of common sense in the confusion that made up her diet. There was the aged notepaper. Surely a rapist would not go to such lengths?—and the severed $1000 bill. Why so much? They could only come from wealth, she decided, hereditary wealth, and that way lay Victorian drawing rooms and a tall dark handsome gentleman who invariably dressed for dinner.

The more Miss Openshaw contemplated Hendrik Brass's invitation, the less perilous became the prospect.

In the end, with excitement in her sharp blue eyes, she decided to take the plunge.

Still, there was no point in being foolhardy. Cornelia Openshaw rose from the sofa and went to her Queen Anne desk. Here, seating herself, she wrote out a check for three months' rent, inserted it in an envelope, addressed, sealed, and stamped the envelope, and deposited it in her purse for immediate mailing. Then she took up a sheet of her Tiffany stationery and poised her pen.

Twenty minutes later, with the wastebasket rich with false starts, she read over the irreducible minimum of her final draft. It said:

If I am not back by the time
my rent next comes due, please
notify the F.B.I. at once.
Cornelia Openshaw

She Scotch-taped the note to the frame of her gilded mirror, attached Hendrik Brass's letter to the mirror, where it would be noticed, packed her alligator suitcase with her frilliest things, notably the lingerie, tucked the whole bill and the bisected bill in her purse, and departed on the dreadful quest.

Like discharged veterans since wars began, Keith Palmer was in a hangup when the letter came. He had had his tour in Vietnam, and the fact that he had come out of it with a whole head was almost beside the point. He could still remember his sweats in the helicopters.

At first they had had him on K.P. at the base five miles from Danang, which was a ball, except for occasional night mortar attacks by Charlie, when you couldn't see a thing except the explosions. Then, with entrenched military logic, they had made him a machine gunner in the birds without a single flight in training. Thereafter it was one crash landing after another. There had been a sort of logic in that, because Keith had come into the service from the junk and scrap iron business. But it was too beautifully logical to have been anything but a coincidence.

One thing, though, they hadn't got him scrubbed. He had won a sprained ankle in one crash, and once he had come down the sole survivor of the crew and been picked up by a rescue craft in exactly sixteen minutes; but that was all. Four of the men with whom he had gone through boot in Tennessee had been shipped back to the States in flag-draped boxes, one had returned an amputee, and one had contracted V.D. during R. and R. in Hong Kong. All Keith had come back with was his life. Of course, there was Joanne waiting, and little Schmulie, as Bill Perlberg called him; but they were another story.

The hangup was that, after Vietnam and the crashing birds, the scrap iron business lost its charm and nothing appeared to take its place. There was a kaleidoscopic succession of stupid jobs, and even one interlude when he hid himself in a freight car headed for nowhere, wife and child notwithstanding (after that one Joanne said, making with the chin, that the next time it happened *she* would take off, with little Sam, and not in any freight car, either); so it had not been all beer and pretzels. What to do? That was Keith's preoccupation when the letter came from Phillipskill, New York.

He fingered the crackling C-note and the scissored $1000 bill unbelievingly as he sat in the dinky office over whose front door the *Palmer & Perlberg* sign still waved (Bill, his ex-partner, had come back from Vietnam to the firm still hoping). Keith had dropped in on Bill expressly to show him Hendrik Brass's letter, and also because it was a dismal Saturday morning and Joanne was home and he had changed Schmulie's diaper six times and Joanne was in one of her I-dare-you-to-start-something moods.

"What do you think, Bill?"

Bill was digesting the letter in his slow way. "Reads to me like a kook."

"Not to me," Keith said. Outwardly they were both twenty-five, good clean American boys, the second-squad football team type. "To me it's something out of an English novel."

Bill shook his head. "The Englanders don't throw their dough around. It has to be an American kook. What are you going to do about this?"

"What would you do, Bill?"

"I'm damned if I know. It sounds real cool, but I have our junk business to run."

"I told you it's not mine any more! Anyway—"

"There's two anyways. Joanne and Schmulie. Have you talked this over with the frau?"

"I chickened out. She doesn't know a thing about it."

"Sounds like one hell of a marriage. Why?"

"Because she's a working wife. What do you think we're living on? We can't get by on the few bucks I'm making working for the town on the roads."

"I'd talk to her."

"You're not married to her."

"To anybody," Bill said with fervor, "and don't you forget it."

"I can't just walk out and go chasing after the missing half of a thousand bucks that may be phoney for all I know. Not after that freight train. Or can I?"

"You're beginning to sound like that schmo Hamlet."

"Joanne wouldn't go for another walkout. She thinks I'm an all-around strikeout as it is."

"Then there's your answer."

"On the other hand, how can I ignore it?" Keith said, nursing on his knuckle. "It's such a gorgeous-sounding setup."

"For what? That's the question."

"Sure it's the question. That's what makes it so gorgeous."

"Look, man, you'd better make up your mind."

"That's why I'm talking to you, isn't it?" Keith Palmer asked his best buddy bitterly.

There was a Great Outdoorsy something about Lynn O'Neill, especially when she laughed, which she was doing now. She evoked motion pictures of long chestnut hair blowing in the prairie wind, Conestoga wagons, rifles across long-skirted knees, and horses. She gave off scent clouds of newmown timothy during morning breezes. It was all done with mirrors, because Lynn was a strictly seventh-decade-of-the-century girl. The last time she had been on a horse he had thrown her, cracking three ribs. That's the kind of decade it was.

She was laughing at the time she opened the squarish envelope—not, certainly, at what fell out of it, because that produced a squeal, but at the whole ridiculous notion of buying life insurance. She had nothing against life insurance per se, but she was confidently going to live to be a hundred, or at least fifty, and whom would she leave insurance to, anyway? And if she had been inclined toward that sort of deal, she surely would not dream of buying a policy from Tom, or Dick, or—no—his name was Harry. Harry was a calculating drip. Lynn wouldn't have given him a sale, let alone a date, if he had been the only whole man in Wagon Springs. He had red hairs creeping out of his nose, and a domed head from which protruded the eyes of a cuttlefish, of a nauseatingly poisonous green.

"Hey!" Harry said. "That's U.S. money you're throwing around, Miss O'Neill."

"It just fell out," Lynn said. "Would you excuse me? I don't ordinarily open my mail while listening to people, but this seems so queer I'm dying of curiosity."

"Take your time," Harry said, performing marvels with his skinny neck.

Lynn read Hendrik Brass's letter. She read it a second time. Then she opened her mouth in a perfect O and said, "Oh!" and "Oh, my!" and read it a third time.

"Somebody leave you a bundle?" Harry asked, panting.

"Not exactly," Lynn said. "Not ever exactly. Oh, I don't know what to do about this."

"Allow me," Harry said, and to her astonishment he plucked the two sheets of vellum paper from her hand and began to read the letter.

"Hey," Lynn said, topaz eyes sparkling. "That's my letter."

"My advice is to keep the dough and throw the letter away. Now about this policy—"

"Some other time," Lynn said, and rose.

"Then we'll sleep on this for a while?"

"You sleep on it, Harry" said Lynn, still burned about the letter; and she marched to the door. When she came back, sans Harry, she picked up the $100 bill and the pinked $1000 bill and read the letter for the fourth time. Out West, where men were men, Lynn had acquired plenty of experience fighting off temptation; could this Brass character be on the make? He sounded old, which did not take him off the hook; the old ones were often the stickiest. On the other hand, there was a kind of humorous sweetness about his style that did not seem to fit with advanced lechery. All in all, it might turn out a gas.

What decided Lynn finally was economics. Worry did not form a significant part of her nature, but the need to eat did, and the fact was she had been one of a number of low-seniority employees who had just received their severance pay, along with the usual printed form of regret.

Her geographical distance from Phillipskill, New York—wherever that was—made flying, and even the moribund railroad, a luxury that would deplete her meager savings; she did not know whether $100 would cover the transportation, but she did know that a bus was the cheapest way to travel; so she telephoned the terminal and got facts and figures, and then she set about tying off knots.

Go East, young woman, Lynn O'Neill said to herself as she packed, and see what gives with this Hendrik Brass.

2

WHERE?

Richard and Jessie Queen spanked sedately along in the Mustang.

Jessie had allowed herself one luxury upon changing names: she had traded in her droopy Dodge and bought the new car, which was fire-bucket red, red-bucket-seated, and sported every gadget in Mr. Ford's repertoire. Richard, whose automotive needs until his retirement had been taken care of by the City of New York, greeted the Mustang like an eight-year-old on Christmas morning.

Being an old-fashioned man, he was taking an old-fashioned route, the Saw Mill River Parkway. There was probably a shinier way to go, but the old Saw Mill had served him lo these many years, and by God it would serve him now.

It was a day as crisp as peanut brittle, and the Inspector had to admit that his blood was crackling. The crackle was only a little damped by the small encyclopedia of facts he had collected at the 42nd Street Library and a newspaper morgue of his acquaintance.

"You're thinking," Jessie said accusingly. "What about?"

"These Brass monkeys."

"Then isn't it time to let me in on what you've found out, Richard? Seeing that it's my letter."

"They came from Holland originally, name of van der Bras or van den Bras. Eventually it turned into a double *s*, without the fancy stuff."

Jessie settled herself, snuggling. The queerness of the mystery had long since made simple nosiness turn to alarm. For the hundredth time she counted the blessings of her union with this admirable man. How had she ever lived without him?

"Go on," Jessie said.

The original migration, the admirable man went on, had come two centuries ago. The Brasses had been metalworkers even then. Having arrived in patroon country well-off, it was not long before they were rich; and with their affluence came the purchase of the present estate, which lay between the then small villages of Tarrytown and Phillipskill. They soon outgrew the house. In a few decades it swelled to baronial proportions, with one wing given over entirely to workshops. Inevitably their creations included the use of precious stones. But they became best known for their gold and sterling pieces, and later platinum.

Jim Fiske was reputed to have spent at least five hundred thousand of his legally stolen dollars at The House of Brass on his statuesque companion, Josie Mansfield. Boss Tweed, the story went, lavished almost as much on his daughter for wedding gifts. But on the whole the clientele of The House were respectable monoliths of finance like rufous-nosed old J.P. Morgan the Elder.

"Then these Brasses must be multimillionaires," Jessie said, looking relieved, as if the possession of multimillions gave automatic absolution from wickedness.

The Mustang was galloping now, and the Inspector took time out to admire the Hudson at its loveliest. "Could be," he said. "It's hard to get rid of that kind of money. Although I got the feeling the family went to pot. I do know there's only one Brass left kicking, this Hendrik, at least up in Phillipskill. He's lived there with one servant for more than ten years now. Sort of a hermit existence."

"Just one servant in a place like that?"

"That's what the news story I dug up said. Seems he takes care of the old man and the house, too."

"How old is he?"

"Who, Brass? Must be seventy-six by this time."

"And the two of them rattle around in a *castle*?"

"It's screwier than that, Jessie. Some local people interviewed by the last reporter to nose around claimed the chimneys in most of the layout show no smoke, sometimes in the dead of winter. But they say there's always smoke from the chimney over the workshop wing."

"Sounds like somebody out of the Middle Ages," Jessie said with an uncertain smile. "I'll bet he walks around in a fur gown with little stars all over it, and a skullcap on his head."

"I don't like how any of it sounds," said Richard Queen in his old inspector's voice. "You sure you want to go through with this, Jessie?"

"I feel the same way, Richard." Jessie even managed to shudder, which under the circumstances was not difficult. "But now that we've come so far, it won't hurt to take a peek, will it? We can always say, 'No, thank you,' and leave."

He snorted and began hunting for the Albany Post Road. Eventually he found it, and they bowled along in a thickening silence.

"There it is!" Jessie said suddenly. "That tavern, Richard."

The Old River Inn had come upon them almost by stealth. It was a sprawling structure of weathered stone and brick, with a wooden gallery that sagged like an old woman's abdomen.

"Didn't he say the second turn to the left after passing the Old River Inn?"

"Damned if I know. Better look at the letter."

Jessie looked, and nodded. "Second to the left."

They parted company with the Post Road to plunge into a rapidly aging past. The paving vanished, the road grew unpredictable, clutching trees tried to get at them from both sides; in one place, a sudden wooden bridge took them precariously over black water. It was Sleepy Hollow country, all right. Jessie had not the least trouble imagining the Headless Horseman "in the very witching time of night" in pursuit of a terrified Ichabod Crane on laboring Old Gunpowder.

"Richard, you almost went past! The *first* turnoff, he said. To the right. There, where it says Private Road on the sign."

The Inspector swore and steered into the byroad. There were more carnivorous trees, an ever-narrowing lane, and everything gone to seed; finally, a colicky bend in the road . . . and there it was, a branch of old Europe grafted onto the American landscape.

The House of Brass was made up of a series of nested buildings snuggling into one another like whelps at their dam's teats. The original building was low and long, with fieldstone walls and a shingled upper story capped by a gambrel roof which swooped down in two stages from a high ridgepole; the major slope was pierced by a soldierly line of dormer windows. The gable ends were clapboard; each slope-edge of the roof was staggered in a series of setbacks, looking for all the world like flights of foreshortened steps, as on Washington Irving's Sunnyside.

From this mother house ran a family of ells, each a house in itself, it seemed, each with its own gambrel roof, each part-fieldstone, part-shingle, part-clapboard, even part-brick. Two of the roofs descended into "kickups," either to avoid darkening the windows below or to shed rainwater from the house; they made Jessie think of the turned-up caps on the Old Dutch Cleanser labels. And all over the roofs, like a bumper crop of mushrooms, rose whitewashed chimneys of different heights and shapes, tall, thin, short, squat, all making erect silhouettes against the sky. Each room of this vast dwelling, it appeared, must have its own fireplace. There were at least thirty chimneys.

The front door of the maternal building was strangest of all. It was of solid, blinding brass. Even before they pulled up in the Mustang they could see that the brass was elaborately decorated in a design that made Jessie think of a medieval tapestry. Brass! Of course. Someone—if not Hendrik Brass, then one of his forebears—had exercised a sense of humor in a sort of architectural pun.

Jessie remarked rather happily about this to her husband as they parked, but all she elicited was a grunt. The Inspector's lifelong chase of wickedness had made him suspicious of all deviations from the conventional; the great brass door was only the climax of a whole chapter of deviations, as far as he was concerned; and Jessie sighed, already knowing him well, and wondered if the scowl was going to become a permanent feature of his dear face.

There was no sign of life.

"You know, darling," Jessie said as she got out and stretched the legs her husband admired so, "this must once upon a time have been a charming place."

"Once," her husband said, "upon one hell of a long time!" Everything looked neglected except the brass door, which glittered as if it had been polished to its highest luster only that morning. Even the vines that crawled over the walls were rachitic-looking. And where there must once have been neat Dutch gardens ran a wasteland of weeds.

The Inspector stumped across the blackened red bricks unevenly paving the driveway, seized the king-sized knocker, and let fly. As he waited, he saw that the tapestry-like design on the brass door was really an arrangement of representations of scales, crucibles, the kind of hammers used in goldbeating, graving tools, and the like. Even the knocker was decorated with them.

Jessie, who at that moment was not interested in doors or knockers, hung back, expecting anything and hoping for nothing at all, an excuse to turn round and go away.

But there was something.

It really did jump, that door, springing like a bird into flight. And there—Jessie almost thought of him as It—there he stood . . . whoever he was . . . filling the doorway with little to spare, an outsized figure of a man that would have been majestic if it had not given off an effluvium of not quite human stupidity.

For one awful moment Jessie heard herself giggle. The apparition was too, too much; she could not decide whether he looked like Mary Shelley's monster or Lurch, the butler on the old Addams Family TV show.

In her nursing career Jessie had seen her quota of patients suffering from dysfunction of the pituitary gland, but usually the condition was restricted to enlargement of the bones of the head and the soft parts of the hands and feet, with the rest of the body relatively normal. This man's acromegaly seemed to have invaded all of him. It was not his fault, naturally, but it did not render him peaceable to the eye. Jessie shut hers for a moment to regain her professional poise. When she opened them the man was looking at her over her husband's head.

Oh, dear, Jessie thought, he saw that. And firmly stepped to the Inspector's side, to reassure the man as well as herself.

He had very little forehead, and small, dull, flawed-looking eyes of a scuffed green, like cheap marbles that had scraped about in a boy's pocket. It was his eyes, Jessie decided charitably, that were responsible for his stupid look. He was wearing the traditional striped apron over a dusty black suit, and a little black tie whose knot was almost buried under his prognathous chin. Undoubtedly Hendrik Brass's factotum.

What Richard Queen thought of Hendrik Brass's factotum could not be detected except by an expert. But Jessie, who was rapidly becoming one, thought she heard an I-told-you-so in his voice.

"We're the Queens."

"Queens?" His voice was froggy, with a booming vibrato, rather like the bass note of a piano that had not been tuned in years. A stained paw went into the striped apron and emerged with a stiffish paper—the same kind of paper, Jessie noted, which Brass had used for his invitation.

There is no Queens on here."

He stepped back, clearly intending to shut the door in their faces. "Hold on there," the Inspector said. "I forgot. I mean you ought to have a Sherwood."

"Sherwood?" The green marbles ran over the paper again. "Yes. Jessie Sherwood."

He backed off. Jessie and Richard stepped over the threshold. The giant immediately presented his bulk to Richard.

"Not you," he said. "Her."

"Now just a minute, please," Jessie said. "No, dear, I'll handle this. Mr. Brass evidently didn't know I'd got married. I don't go anywhere my husband can't go. If Mr. Brass wants me, he'll have to take Mr. Queen too. You march right in there and tell Mr. Brass that."

The oversized lips writhed. "I will go and see," he said, and slammed the door. They had to jump back.

"And you still want to go through with this, Jessie?" Richard asked in a dangerously mild voice.

"Oh, Richard, the poor man can't help it. He was born that way. Let's wait and see what Hendrik Brass is like."

"Anybody who'd hire a guy like that to answer doors has to be a chandelier swinger. Take my word for it, you're stepping into something you'll wish you hadn't."

"Now, darling, you promised—"

"This might even turn out risky. That hulk has a hundred and fifty pounds on me."

"He's probably the most harmless man, darling. I've known loads of acromegalics. They're very gentle people."

"And bright?"

"Yes."

"Well, this one isn't. Whatever's in that head of his, it's not brains. I tell you you can't predict what one like that'll do."

"You sound positively bigoted, Richard Queen! Can't we just wait and see?"

The brass door swooshed inward again, startling them.

"Come."

"The two of us?" The Inspector sounded disappointed.

The man nodded and stepped aside.

"You see, Richard?" Jessie said. "Really, I should have let Mr. Brass know you were coming, too. It would only have been good manners."

The Inspector grunted his opinion of good manners, and they stepped into Nieuw Amsterdam. Or what might have been Nieuw Amsterdam if not for the brass.

Brass winked and flashed everywhere. Articles that might have been true specimens of early and Revolutionary Dutch were transformed by it into things neither authentic nor beautiful, only brassified. Brass handles had even been fitted to old hearth hairbrushes and brooms, and they saw a basket whose original wicker was now a mere lining to a brass container.

They were standing in a wide hall that ran the depth of the house. The front parlor was almost wholly visible through the broad doorway at their left. Its dominant feature was a man-tall fireplace with a brass mantelpiece and brass side-pieces; only practical considerations, they felt, had kept their brass-mad host from plating the old Dutch firebrick and the black iron door to the Dutch oven. But the fire tools were of brass, and so was the wood box.

Brass's man, who had suddenly named himself Hugo, had gone out to the Mustang for their luggage; now, with a bag under each gorilla arm, he nodded at them and led the way to the staircase. It was of the Dutch boxed-in type, dating from the time when the upper floors were used for the storage of provisions, hay, and spinning and weaving materials and consequently did not, in the burgher's view, require heating; the boxing was, of course, laminated with sheets of brass. What had probably been a mahogany handrail had been replaced with a brass one; the original delicate spindles were now brass as well. On the steps, screwed down, were brass foot-plates showing the scratching of many years of use. And what were evidently ancestral portraits, primitives by justifiably forgotten artists, showing patroon and *goede vrouw* faces overlaid with hairnets of fine paint-cracks, marched up the stairwell in step with the risers, each portrait massively reframed in ornamented brass.

The hall upstairs was a cramped place with shadowy crooks where it angled off into the ells; the whole thing boded Tom Thumb bedrooms. Nor were they disappointed. As they followed Hugo past open doorways—some doors were shut—they saw into empty, dim, tiny bedrooms remarkable only for their brassy interiors—doorknobs, beds, lamps, fireplace tools, candlesticks, sconces, snuffers, clock pendulums, cornices, and chandeliers (some of which had been converted to electricity; others were still fitted with gas mantles)—all, all of brass.

Hugo kicked open a door and stumped through, jerking his great head in a follow-me signal, and they found themselves in a miniature sitting room paneled from floor to ceiling in brass, the metal covered with the same designs they had seen on the front door. The little room was furnished with falling-apart Dutch settle-like pieces. The chairs looked as uncompromising as pews.

The giant edged through another doorway which made him stoop, and dropped their bags, the Queens following dumbly into a bedroom. The room looked crowded, as much because it was overfurnished as undersized. The same worn-down furniture was everywhere.

The brass double bed was swollen with featherbedding that looked soft but not quite clean. Nothing looked quite clean. Jessie's heart sank. A few courageous rays of sun managed to get through the dormer-window shutters, which were of the Dutch batten type, with saw-cut openings in the shape of half moons, hearts, and pots of flowers.

To Jessie's relief, the brass chandelier was electrified. At least they would not go blind if they wanted to read something at bedtime. But when she looked around, there wasn't a book to be seen, nor even a magazine. And they hadn't thought to bring any reading matter. Oh, well, Jessie thought, I'll cross that bridge when Richard gets to it.

In one corner lay a huge can of brass polish and a pile of dirty rags. Hugo had apparently been interrupted by their arrival.

"You must buy polish by the case lots, Hugo," Richard Queen remarked with menacing softness. "What is this brass thing with Mr. Brass?"

"I," Hugo said proudly, "made the brass."

"You? Made all of it?"

"Most. Mr. Hendrik taught me. Down there," the long arm descended like an ax, "in the workshop."

"Well, I'll be," the Inspector said. "Okay. When do we get to see your Mr. Hendrik?"

Hugo shook his improbable head. "I am to answer no questions. Mr. Hendrik said to say he would see you all later this afternoon. Meantime you are to unpack and rest."

"See us *all?* All who?"

"All Mr. Hendrik's guests. You are the last."

"How many of us are there? I didn't see any cars outside."

"I have put them in the coach house. I will put yours away, too. Key?" The impossible hand reached.

The Inspector looked stubborn. But then, catching a wifely glance, he handed over the ignition key. Hugo scooped up the rags and polish and left.

Husband and wife engaged in a duel of stares. Jessie decided on a strategic diversion. "Goodness, a girl needs a bathroom. I'd hate to have to use an outhouse," and she investigated another door, which she knew perfectly well must lead to a bathroom, as it indeed did—a surprisingly large one, with a ceiling that made her feel like whoever had been down in the Pit while the Pendulum swung, and with an old room-sized tub replated in brass down to its claw feet, and brass fittings everywhere. She shut the door, wishing she had been married long enough to get over the traditional embarrassments.

Richard hung about outside. "Blast it all, Jessie, the more I see of this setup the less I like it. What do you say? Be a good girl and let's get the hell out of here."

"Without even meeting Mr. Brass?" Jessie said through the door. "Richard." What Richard responded was drowned by the plumbing.

When she came out he was stooped over the nearest leg of the bedstead. "Look at this," he muttered. "The damn bed legs are *screwed* to the floor. I told you this Brass is off his rocker."

"Oh, hush. You know, considering how old this house must be, it's in wonderful condition. The floors don't sag at all. And the ceiling looks so sturdy. . . ." She wanted to mollify him, so she dropped that line and said instead, "But it *is* on the gloomy side."

"You're damn tootin' it is!"

"Do you have to swear about everything, dear?" Jessie sat down on the bed. She sank deep into the ancient counterpane and simultaneously raised a splash of dust. "Whoo! We can't sleep in this, Richard. You throw open those shutters and windows, and I'll dust and air the bed things, and . . . What are you doing *now*?"

He was wrestling with a walleyed female van den Bras framed in the ubiquitous brass. He wrestled in vain. "The painting is screwed down, too!"

"I know, dear, I know," Jessie said in the tone she had employed with young women in labor, although she hadn't noticed the screws in the wall at all; and she got him busy with the windows to take his mind off Hendrik Brass.

But the first thing Richard saw when he opened a shutter was their Mustang disappearing with a weird finality, as if driving itself, behind the farthest ell.

It struck another portentous note.

What sort of place had they got themselves into?

3

WHY?

Jessie was stretched out on the aired and cleaned bed when the brazen thunderclap came. She had removed her dress and slipped into one of her trousseau negligees, but the filmy stuff had parted when she turned over in the doze, and Richard was standing over her admiring her C-cups, the length of her lashes, and her other remarkable attributes. The crash made her eyes fly open in telltale terror, and brought him around to the door with an agility that would have done credit to a man half his age.

"What in the world was *that*?" Jessie whispered.

The Inspector uncoiled. "A Chinese gong. Brass, what else? I have a hunch we're about to meet Chief Hazelnut himself."

"Everyone in the parlor!" Hugo was roaring.

When they got downstairs they found six people assembled. Hugo had vanished.

The Inspector took inventory. None of the three men present was old enough to be Hendrik Brass. One—large and formidable-looking, with a country squire's complexion and unblinking little eyes—might have been taken for sixty by the innocent; but to the Inspector, who had sized men up for a living, the red-faced man was considerably younger; a hard and shabby life had left its premature mark on his flesh. The second male of the sextet, a stooped and skinny six-footer with a red mustache, wearing horn rims one shaft of which was taped with adhesive, was no more than middle-aged. The third, with the physique of an inactive football player, was in his late or mid-twenties.

Jessie paid more attention to the three women. The one seated in the chair behind which the country squire was standing made her feel uncomfortable on sight. She was in her forties, slim and elegant, the elegance ever so slightly tarnished, with an imperious tilt to her too perfectly coifed, dyed brown-blonde hair and a deadly quiet something in her face. Jessie knew intuitively that they made a pair, legal or otherwise. She did not like them at all.

The second woman, in her late thirties, was so heavily made up that she looked grotesque. Her swift appraisal of Richard as they came in, and her equally swift dismissal of him, made Jessie want to slap her face. The creature immediately went back to what she had evidently been doing before their entrance, devouring the footballish young man with her dental eyes. Jessie put her down as Inhibited Female, probably Spinster, and unquestionably Man-crazy.

The third woman was no more than a girl. Jessie decided to like her. She was pretty, with a fresh look, topaz eyes of spirit, and a pile of natural chestnut hair that begged to be shaken out and brushed. The young man of the group was showing signs of interest; and from the way the girl ignored him Jessie knew that she was pleasantly aware of his interest.

"Welcome to the club," the young man said, advancing with outstretched hand. "I saw you people drive up from my window. My name is Keith Palmer."

"Richard Queen," the Inspector said, shaking Palmer's hand with a vigor that told Jessie the young man had passed muster. "My wife Jessie."

"Mrs. Queen. May I present Mr. and Mrs. Alistair?" He indicated the deadly woman in the far chair and the florid man behind her. "Miss Cornelia Openshaw"—that was Miss Hot-Pants, Jessie nodded to herself, and unmarried as deduced. "Miss Lynn O'Neill"—the fresh-faced girl. "And Dr. Hubert Thornton." And that was the tall stooped man with the broken shaft. "You folks wouldn't know what this is all about, would you?"

The Inspector shook his head. "My wife got a letter from this Brass with money and instructions in it, and that's all we know."

"We all did," young Lynn O'Neill said. "We've compared letters, and they're identical except for the addresses."

"Did anybody here *know* anybody else before today?" Jessie asked.

There was a general disclaimer.

"I don't know why I came." Dr. Thornton lit a cigaret from the end of a butt and tossed the butt into the cave of the fireplace, where a monumental log was blazing away. "The whole thing sounds like the product of hardened arteries to me. I ought to turn around and drive back to South Cornwall."

"Not so smart," Alistair said from behind his wife's chair. He was all smiles, all but his eyes. "There's money in this, and who can't use money?"

Mrs. Alistair said nothing. She's the one to watch, the Inspector decided. She's not so sure there's money in it, but if there is it will be a tossup as to who grabs first, she or her husband.

"Anybody else coming, do you know?" he asked.

"Hugo says we're the lot," Palmer said. "Where is this Brass, anyway? Letting us stew this way."

"Old trick," Mrs. Alistair said suddenly. Then her linear lips clamped shut, as if she had caught herself in an indiscretion.

"Here's Hugo," Lynn O'Neill said, cocking her head. "Who else would sound like the Giant in Jack and the Beanstalk?"

"I wonder what Mr. Brass looks like," Miss Openshaw wondered thoughtfully.

All heads swiveled.

Hugo appeared, a gigantic illusion.

Clinging to his arm was a miniaturized ancient with twiggy arms and legs and a little gray face whose nose seemed bent on making contact with his pointy chin. The face was connected to the shoulders by a long neck that did not look as if it had the strength to support the head. He carried a brass cane that quivered; and he was wearing a faded red velvet jacket with brocaded lapels, a woolen scarf about his shoulders shot with moth holes, and old carpet slippers on his feet. The few white hairs on his bone of a skull were at attention, like the gallant remnants of a defeated regiment.

But the most remarkable thing about Hendrik Brass's appearance was his eyes, or rather the absence of them. They were invisible behind dark glasses of coy, extreme design, more fitting for a bikini-clad beach girl. They concealed half his little face.

"Well, well," Hendrik Brass chirped. And indeed his voice, like the rest of him, made them think of an aged bird. "Are they all here, Hugo?" He seemed to peer.

"Yes, Mister Hendrik."

"Good. I am going to call your names, my friends. Please answer to them." Calling a *roll*? "Mr. Alistair."

"Here," Alistair said at once.

"No, Mr. Alistair, say something more. Repeat your name."

"My name is DeWitt Alistair. Is that all right?"

Brass nodded, and the brass cane twitched. "I believe your wife is with you, sir?"

"My name is Elizabeth Alistair," said Mrs. Alistair. She was staring at him as if she were puzzled.

"Dr. Thornton."

The red-mustached doctor said, "I'm Hubert Thornton, Mr. Brass." He was looking puzzled, too, but it was the puzzlement of a clinician with a problem.

"Miss Cornelia Openshaw? Mr. Keith Palmer? Miss Lynn O'Neill? Miss Jessie Sherwood?—I beg your pardon, Mrs. Richard Queen, I understand. And Mr. Queen?" One by one they humored him. "Good, good, you've all come. Couldn't resist, eh? Well, you'll find out what this is all about right now. I didn't mean it to sound mysterious." He cheeped, and it was as if a sparrow had burst into laughter—a rather wicked sparrow, Jessie thought emotionally. "Hugo, you oaf, are you going to let me stand here forever? My chair."

Hugo rushed over to the fireplace, plucked an overstuffed paterfamilias chair of elaborate design (some of the stuffing, Jessie noticed, was coming out) with one hand, and rushed it back to the doorway.

He set it precisely behind the old man, and Hendrik Brass sat himself on the edge of it, gripping his cane between his bony knees. In this position he was facing all of them, but he seemed to be staring into the fire rather than at them, because his head did not move at all during what followed, even when someone spoke.

"It is really a simple matter," he began. "I am the only survivor of the Brass family. I have no heirs. I'm old, I'm sick, and I'm rich. Six million dollars rich. You hear me? Six million. I'd be worth a great deal more," he said with a vicious little tweet, "if the government didn't take big chunks of it and give it away to a lot of greedy foreigners. I'll be damned if I'll let 'em have all of it when I die."

Hugo stood guard behind the armchair, one hand on it as if to be ready should it fall apart suddenly, as indeed it looked as though it might. No one said anything at this point. The $6,000,000 confidence took savoring. Keith Palmer looked incredulous, Dr. Thornton thoughtful, Miss Openshaw delighted, Lynn O'Neill astounded; only the Alistairs retained their sniffy expressions, as if testing the wind and unwilling to believe the evidence of their noses.

"So," continued Hendrik Brass with a smack of his little blue lips. "Of you eight, I have sought out six—you, Mrs. Alistair, and you, Mr. Queen, are here only because of your spouses. Actually, my friends, I set out to locate nine people. My information now is that two of them are dead, and no trace could be found of the ninth, a certain Harding Boyle. Do you follow me?"

He tilted his head at this. There was a general mumble, none of it projectile. What could anyone sensibly say? The old man was either in a high flight of paranoia, or he was pulling their collective legs in a senile joke. The property must once have been impressive, but everything they had seen so far was racked and riddled with age and neglect. To think of this seedy little septuagenarian in his motheaten scarf and worn-down carpet slippers as the possessor of $6,000,000 called for absolute faith.

"Now why did I pick you six out of two hundred million people to stand in line for my money?" their host went on. "Good question? The one you're asking yourselves? I'll tell you why. The reason, my friends, is that each of you is either the son or daughter of someone who gave me a helping hand during a crisis in my life. And yet none of you has ever heard of me. Right? Speak up."

No one spoke up. They were so many children with bubble-gum balloons at their mouths, afraid to breathe and so burst them. There was a fantastic something about Hendrik Brass and his chirping, no doubt helped out by the enormous flicker of the fire and the glitter of the overpowering brass, that made the old Dutch parlor seem like a stage set and everyone in it a character in a play, with Brass its author-producer-director.

Old Hendrik apparently took their silence for applause. "Am I right, too, that your parents are all dead? I'm told they are, or I promise you I'd have had them here instead of you. The virtues of the fathers shall be visited upon the children, eh?" He smacked his lips at his wit.

And DeWitt Alistair said suddenly, as if he had made up his mind to leap a dangerous gap, "Mr. Brass."

"That would be Mr. Alistair," the old man said, staring

into his fire; and the Inspector solved one of the mysteries and was irritated with himself. Hendrik Brass was blind. He should have realized it at once from the cane, the dark glasses, the fixity of the old man's head, and his having made each of them say something. "Yes, Mr. Alistair?"

The big man said smoothly, in his thunky voice, "You refer to the six of us as 'standing in line' for your money. What d'ye mean by that?"

"You stand in line, Mr. Alistair, you're waiting. And you don't know if you're going to get to the teller's window before it closes. I may decide to leave my fortune to one of you, or two of you, or all of you, or maybe none of you. Depends."

"On what, Mr. Brass?" Cornelia Openshaw asked suspiciously.

"Just be yourselves is my advice, Miss Openshaw. I warn you, I'm a hard man to diddle."

He flourished his cane, and the firelight caught its brass like a sword.

"Since none of you knows me, or what my connection was with one or both of your parents, I'll tell you." He stabbed with the cane in Jessie's direction. "You, Jessie Sherwood—excuse me, Mrs. Queen—your father was a medical doctor. Dr. Sherwood's skill saved my life when I was very sick. I've never forgotten."

Jessie looked startled. She was about to say something when Richard's pressure on her shoulder stopped her.

"In your case, Dr. Thornton, it was—bless her—your mother. At the lowest time of my life she hauled me to my feet again, restored my confidence in myself. If you're half the man your mother was a woman, Doctor, you're going to be a lucky fellow.

"Mr. Alistair," the old man continued, "it's my pleasure to inform you that one time when I was deep in financial difficulties and had exhausted every possible source of help, your father lent me money I needed. Of course I repaid the debt, but I can never forget that he came to my rescue when everyone else turned me down."

The con man looked profoundly astonished; and the Inspector only a little less so.

"Miss O'Neill," Brass said to the pretty girl, "I spent some years in the West at one time in my life, and it turned out I was accused of stealing a horse. The sheriff saved me from lynching. What's more, he saw to it I got a fair trial—in fact, proved I was not guilty and had to go against public opinion to do it. That sheriff, Miss O'Neill, was your father. I could hardly do less than remember him with gratitude."

Lynn O'Neill frowned. But she was silent.

"Keith Palmer." The old man hesitated. "No, I'd best not go into details in your mother's case. Our—well, friendship—meant a great deal to me, a great deal. Let's let it go at that."

"Whatever you say, Mr. Brass," Keith said. The Inspector grinned to himself. Palmer was trying to visualize the old gnome as a young blade seducing a fair maiden, and he was clearly having trouble doing it.

"And that leaves you, Miss Openshaw."

"Yes? Yes?" Cornelia Openshaw said, open-mouthed.

"When I was a young man, I went through a period of extreme depression. I was determined to commit suicide. I actually tried to. Your parents saved my life. A man doesn't forget people like that, even after half a century."

Miss Openshaw turned misty-eyed. "I had a very wonderful father," she said.

Hendrik's old head nodded. They waited. Finally he stirred. "So that's why I've had you all come. . . ."

"For how long, Mr. Brass?" Alistair demanded.

"For as long as I need to make up my mind about you. Testing period, you might say. I'll be watching you all, and I don't need years for that. You're free to leave at any time, of course, and when you do—whether it's before I'm ready or not—you'll at least get the missing half of the thousand dollar bill. You understand that if any of you should leave before I've made a decision, you can forget about sharing in my estate. A gamble worth at least a sixth of six million dollars ought to be worth the investment of a few weeks' time."

"And when you've decided?" Elizabeth Alistair said.

"Then, Mrs. Alistair, I'll make my will. Meanwhile, my friends, we'll try to make you as comfortable as this old place will allow. I'm having some extra day help come in, and Hugo will be doing the cooking. You ask him for whatever you want. Well. well," Hendrik Brass said irritably, "get me up, Hugo! All this talk has tuckered me. Hugo, do you hear, idiot?"

He turned in the paterfamilias chair and lashed out with the cane. Hugo paid no more attention to the blows than if they had been delivered with jackstraws. He hauled the old man gently to his feet; and then, huge jaw hanging, he led his master away like a gigantic hound, out of the parlor and up the staircase, until the sideshow pair disappeared from view.

The Scotch broth was almost cold, the pork was under-done, and the vegetables were cooked to a fare-thee-well.

"If tonight was typical of Hugo's cooking," the Inspector grumbled when he and Jessie finally escaped to their rooms, "we'll die of dyspepsia before that old curlicue makes up his mind. I'm going to have to stock up on milk of magnesia."

"Richard," Jessie said. She sounded so unhappy that he turned in alarm. "There's something I have to tell you."

"I knew it," he exclaimed. "I knew it the minute he talked to you!"

"To tell the truth, I don't know what to make of this. There's been some mistake."

"What mistake, Jessie?"

"Richard, my father never was a doctor. He was a civil service employee all his life—worked in the post office till the day he retired. I was just going to tell that to Mr. Brass when you stopped me."

"A mixup," he muttered. "Whoever did old Brass's tracking for him located the wrong Jessie Sherwood—it's not that uncommon a name. It makes me wonder . . ."

"What, Richard?"

"If you're the only one."

Jessie stared. "You mean others of these people may be the wrong ones, too?"

"Why not? If your case is a sample, no one ever bothered to interview the people Brass wanted found. Sounds to me like a hurry-up job by somebody who didn't give a damn. How would the old man know the difference? Another thing. How come the Harding Boyle that the old boy mentioned wasn't located at all? This is starting to get interesting."

"Oh, you and your—your coppiness," Jessie moaned. "The question is, what do I *do*? I don't see any way out of it. I'll have to tell Mr. Brass I'm not the Jessie Sherwood he's looking for."

"Well, sure," the Inspector said; he was tugging at his ear. "But does it have to be right now?"

"You mean we're to stay on in spite of—?"

"There's something rotten about this setup, Jessie. I'd like to know what it is."

"I simply don't understand you! First you didn't want me to come. Then when I did, you pestered me to leave. And now that you know I have no right to be here at all, you want me to stay!"

"Can't a man change his mind? Honey, you look beat. Why don't you go to bed?"

"And what are you going to do?"

The Inspector managed to look and sound remarkably like his remote son. "Think."

Jessie flounced into the bathroom.

Richard Queen seized the opportunity, stealthily, while she was out of sight and hearing, to lock and bolt their doors.

The featherbed was so deeply demoralizing that sleep came late and wakefulness early. The Inspector, who had the habits of a monk, was used to a hard mattress; and Jessie had had to massage too many aching backs to approve of a soft one. With dawn prying at their eyes, Jessie thinking Richard asleep and Richard thinking Jessie asleep, each had turned noiselessly over so as not to disturb the other, when disturbance would have been a relief.

So they were both fully awake and on their feet at opposite sides of the bed, even though it was two hours later, before the echo of the first shriek died away. The shriek, a woman's, was followed quickly by a muffled shouting that they realized had been going on for some time; that was followed by a ponderous running and stumbling about that they now recalled had anticipated the shriek as well. Then there was the second shriek in the same female timbre, and a thud, sex indeterminable.

"I knew it!" Richard snarled, although what it was he had known he did not explain, even to himself. He grabbed his robe. "Jessie, lock the door after me—"

"Not on your life," Jessie panted, grabbing, too. "You're not leaving me in here alone, Richard Queen!"

He went first, shoving her behind him and holding her there. He had an impression of disheveled heads protruding from doorways and peering around the ells at the ends of the hall; but it was no more than a camera flash, because it was immediately shut out by the sight and sound of Hugo thundering up and down the hall like a bull elephant in musth, trumpeting, "He is dead! Dead! Ah, help, help!" while his extraordinary features worked in all directions, totally disorganized. The source of the thud they quickly identified. Miss Openshaw was lying across the threshold of her room in a sheer black nightgown that half revealed her virgin udders; her eyes were shut and the hairnet she had slept in had slipped down over one of them; her lips and what could be seen of her chunky legs were on the blue side. Young Palmer, in pajamas, fortunately opaque, knelt by her, slapping her cheek with one hand and trying to stop Hugo with the other as the giant crashed past. (They learned later that Miss Openshaw had opened her door at Hugo's bellow, caught the word "dead," shrieked, asked who was dead, was answered, shrieked again, and fainted.)

It was Hendrik Brass, it seemed, who was dead. The Inspector, who had jumped out into Hugo's path and stopped him by sheer force of character, was able to elicit that much and no more.

"Where's that doctor?" the Inspector roared.

Dr. Thornton appeared from one of the ell corridors. He had thrown a topcoat over his nightshirt, and he had a wild look in his eye.

"What now, for heaven's sake?"

"Hugo says old Brass is dead. You'd better come with me." The Inspector stopped. "Come where?" he demanded of the Almighty. "I don't even know where he beds down! Hugo, where's Mr. Brass's room?"

Hugo gaped at him.

"I know where it is." DeWitt Alistair began to run. He stopped very short opposite the landing. "It's in there." He made no move to follow the stab of his meaty forefinger.

Mrs. Alistair hovered somewhere in the background, intent as a cat on a tree; she wore a threadbare, slickly ironed black flannel robe and gold bedroom slippers with some of the gold threads missing. Lynn O'Neill and Jessie were helping Cornelia Openshaw to her feet; the spinster shrank against them at the sight of poor Hugo, who seemed in shock. Keith Palmer ran down the hall toward the Inspector and Dr. Thornton to see what had to be seen.

They were blinded by brass; and then they wheeled on the old man in the bed. He was lying askew on a bloody pillow; his sunken eyes were shut; his face was grayer than gray where it was not scarlet. Dr. Thornton plucked the twiggy hand from the coverlet, feeling for the artery.

Hugo croaked from the doorway, "He is dead, dead," a froggy requiem, deep and dolorous, conveying fundamental distress.

The doctor looked up. "No such thing," he said sharply. "There's a good pulse." His glance swept professionally over the still bleeding head. "Somebody fetch my medical bag from the garage. It's on the back seat of my car." Young Palmer said quickly, "I'll do it, Doctor," and vaulted down the stairs. "And one of you women get some hot water."

Jessie said from the doorway, "You do it, Miss O'Neill. I can be more useful here," and she came in and said, "I'm a registered nurse, Doctor," as calm as a barge on a windless day; and Richard felt a fine warmth. Then he got busy using his eyes.

The bedroom was very like the room they had been assigned, full of decrepit furniture, only brassier if that was possible. There was a fireplace with a profusion of brass fire tools; it was faced with Dutch tiles that were cracked and faded-looking. But he was not concerned with the condition of Hendrik Brass's heirlooms. He was trying to make a different assessment.

When Palmer returned with the black bag, the doctor was carefully going over the old man's head. Jessie seized the bag and began pulling things out, anticipating Dr. Thornton's needs; they worked in silence.

Lynn O'Neill came in with a steaming kettle. Jessie took it from her and shooed the girl out. At that moment she caught sight of her husband. "What are you *doing,* Richard?"

He was on his knees, lean rump uppermost, near the foot of Brass's bed, delicately raising the corner of the pulled-over coverlet, which showed smears of blood.

"Here's what did it." There was a long brass poker on the floor, half under the bed. The tip looked as if it had been dipped in strawberry jam. He glanced over at the fireplace; the poker was missing from the rack of fire tools. "He was hit over the head, probably in his sleep. How many wounds are there, Doctor?"

"Three. The only reason he's alive is that the pillow must have taken most of the force of the blows. He looks in a lot worse shape than he actually is. These scalp wounds can be messy."

"Any skull fracture?"

"Not that I can see. By God, the old fellow is all ready to come around. He's either got the constitution of a horse or he was born under a lucky star."

The sightless eyes were beginning to flutter under the pain of Dr. Thornton's stitching.

"Don't anybody touch that poker. Hugo, what happened?" The Inspector had to repeat himself. Hugo shook like a dog.

"I bring Mr. Hendrik breakfast in bed every morning. I found him all full of blood. I thought—he looked—"

The Inspector nodded. "Where's the telephone?"

"No phone. Mr. Hendrik does not like them."

"He wouldn't." The Inspector started for the door.

"What do you want a telephone for, Richard?" Jessie was swabbing the blood from the old man's face as Dr. Thornton bandaged the bald head.

"I have to make a call." He shook his head at her, and she nodded in wifely understanding. What a team we'd have made twenty-five years ago! he thought. "Better make sure nobody touches anything."

He went out, shutting the door, and began to push through. To their questions he merely said, "He's not dead. Had an accident," and went to his and Jessie's bedroom, where he rapidly dressed. Then he hurried around to the old converted coach house, retrieved the Mustang, and drove out of the grounds and back the way they had come the day before, to pull up at the Old River Inn. It was still not open for the day, but he located a public booth at one side of the building.

"Get me the Phillipskill police," he said to the operator. When he was connected he said, "I'm reporting an assault on Mr. Hendrik Brass," gave his name, made a suggestion, hung up, went out, got into the Mustang, and drove back looking grim.

Incredibly, he found the old man sitting up in bed, demanding his breakfast. Brass had put his dark glasses on, and with his bandaged head he looked like some ancient delinquent who had just taken part in a rumble. Dr. Thornton and Jessie were trying to reason with him, and the argument about his breakfast, which they lost, was succeeded by his absolute refusal to hear another word about Thornton's recommendation that he check into the nearest hospital for head X-rays and observation for possible concussion.

Richard left them arguing, to slip out of the house and look around. He was still checking doors and windows when a police car drove up and two uniformed men got out. One was carrying a fingerprinting kit, and the other wore a chief's badge on his blue coat.

"Are you the man who phoned headquarters?" the chief's badge demanded. He was a burly, farmerish sort with a red face and a big belly. "I'm Chief Victor Fleck."

The Inspector nodded. "I'm Richard Queen. Retired police inspector from New York City."

Chief Fleck did not seem overjoyed by the news. "What are you doing here?"

The Inspector told him, and ran down Hendrik Brass's guest list and the story of the morning's events. "My guess is that whoever clobbered him thought he'd killed the old man. He hit him three times, and there was blood all over him and the bed; he looked dead enough. In my book it was attempted murder."

Fleck grunted. "Doesn't surprise me. Everything the old screwball does, from the stories, is way out."

"Ever been in the house, Chief?"

"No."

"It's a doozy," the Inspector said.

"Before I go in, Queen. You understand that, even if you weren't retired, you'd have no jurisdiction here? Far as I'm concerned, this case is my case and you're just another character named Joe, up to and including being a suspect. Right?"

"Right."

"But as long as we're talking—was anything taken? Could this have been a burglary?"

"I don't know. Dr. Thornton just brought the old man to, and I haven't had a chance to question him." The inspector kept a straight face.

"What were you doing when I drove up? I mean out here."

"Looking for signs of forcible entry. There aren't any."

"Inside job?"

"Looks like it to me."

"Any idea who?"

Richard shook his head. "Not a notion." Something told him that the likeliest candidate for the assault was DeWitt Alistair, but it was only a hunch. Let Fleck find out, if he were capable of it. He had met Flecks before. These small town chiefs were usually over their heads in anything more complicated than a hit-and-run.

"Oh, one other thing," Chief Fleck said, turning at the door. "Why your suggestion about bringing fingerprint equipment?"

"The poker," Richard Queen said gently.

"Oh," Fleck said; and they all went into the house.

They found Hugo fork-feeding the old man from a loaded tray. The Inspector recalled Brass's statement that he was a sick man. Sick with what? It could have nothing to do with his digestion. There was a half-inch slab of ham cut into small pieces, three fried eggs, a mound of buttered toast, and a pot of coffee; and the recipient of all this waited greedily between forkfuls, making sucking sounds.

Jessie and Dr. Thornton hovered, unbelieving.

At the tramp of the three men Brass stopped in midchomp.

"Who is that?" he mumbled. "There are three of you."

"It's Queen, Mr. Brass," the Inspector said. "I've got Chief Fleck of the Phillipskill police and one of his officers with me."

"You've got *who*?" Hendrik Brass wheezed, spitting egg. "Who authorized you to call the police? Get them out of my house!"

"Mr. Brass," the Inspector said, startled, "somebody tried to kill you."

"And whose business is that? If I want police I'll call 'em. My family's lived on this property for two hundred years and never once asked anybody for help—anybody from the *government*!—not even during the Rent Wars. Get 'em out!"

"Now just a minute, Mr. Brass," said Chief Fleck, man-to-man. "If you've been assaulted, it's my job to come in on it—"

"Who said I was assaulted?"

"Why, this man here. Queen."

"And what's he know about it? Did he see it happen?"

"That poker didn't hit you over the head by itself, Mr. Brass," the Inspector said. "Unless you did it yourself?"

To their amazement the old man heehawed. "Yes, sir, that's what happened, all righty, I hit myself over the head. And you prove I didn't." He screamed suddenly, "Get out, I said! Off my property!"

Hugo hastily put some ham into his mouth.

Chief Fleck had turned beef-colored. Dr. Thornton hurried over and whispered, "My advice is to drop this for now, gentlemen. At least leave the room. There might be a concussion, and he shouldn't be excited."

"You the doctor Queen told me about?"

"I'm Dr. Thornton."

"They why don't you sign a commitment paper for the old birdseed? Anybody can see his brain's gone to jelly. You through with that poker, Bobby?"

The officer set the poker down and put his equipment away. "No prints, Vic. Must have been wiped."

"The hell with this." Fleck raised his voice. "Look, Mr. Brass, I was called here and I've got to put something down for the record. You're not going to press a charge against anybody, or make a complaint?"

"That's it."

"It's all right with me." The chief nodded curtly at the Inspector, who followed him and his man into the hall. "This isn't the end of it by a long shot, Queen. You know it and I know it."

"I'm afraid I do."

"If he denies an assault and won't lodge a complaint, I can't do anything. But if something else happens to him I want to be notified. Understood?"

"For two cents plain," muttered the Inspector, "I'd chuck the whole thing."

"Then you're not staying? Can't stop you."

The Inspector shrugged. "You know I am. I haven't any idea what my wife and I are mixed up in here, but I'm still enough of a cop to want to find out."

"What I thought," Chief Fleck said with a heavy grin. "And that's why I'm warning you, Queen. Something happens here, I'm not standing by and watch some ex-New York cop grab off all the publicity. Like I said, this is my neck of the woods."

"Whatever happens, Chief," Richard said solemnly, "I promise you: you can talk to the reporters."

The burly policeman seemed to detect a whiff of irony. "Okay, Queen," he said gruffly, "as long as we understand each other." The officers clumped downstairs, and a moment later he heard the police car peel off.

The Inspector went back into the bedroom. Dr. Thornton was filling a hypodermic, and Jessie was dabbing the old man's spindly arm. Hugo was preparing to leave with the tray, and the Inspector took it from him. "I'll take this downstairs. I have a job for you."

Hugo looked stupid.

"You know somebody tried to hurt Mr. Hendrik?"

The massive head wagged.

"Well, the job I want you to do, Hugo, is to keep watch over him. So nobody can get near him to hurt him again. Know what I mean? Don't leave this room, not for a second. If there's anything funny, yell."

"The cooking—" began Hugo.

"The women can take care of that."

Hugo looked torn. But then he nodded.

Jessie took the tray from Richard, and he followed her and Dr. Thornton out. The last thing he saw before he shut the door was Hugo settling down at the foot of the brass bed, little eyes fixed on his master's face.

While Jessie dressed, the Inspector slipped downstairs for a cup of coffee and a few minutes alone with his thoughts.

He was enormously puzzled. The assault on Hendrik Brass made no sense. According to Brass he had not yet drawn a will. He had certainly not chosen his heir or heirs; the whole point of his invitations was to enable him to weigh the chosen six in the balance and cull the unworthy from among them, a procedure that had barely got under way. Old Brass had mentioned "weeks."

Why had someone—presumably someone in the house—attempted to kill off the goose before it could lay the egg? The only beneficiary, had the murder attempt succeeded, would have been the treasury of the State of New York.

Yet it must make sense of some sort. Unless the assailant was as off-balance as Hendrik himself, there was a motive hidden somewhere that related to at least one of the guests. A motive that was stronger than $1,000,000.

He tried to imagine such a motive. Maybe one of them was loaded—so loaded that $1,000,000 meant little to him; one man's million was another man's spending money. But, thinking over the five people besides Jessie who were involved, he could not see any of them so fortunately situated.

Barring that, the Inspector thought wryly, whoever did it is a nut, like old Hendrik himself. Nuts made no sense except to other nuts. It was the only explanation, unsatisfactory as it was, that he could think of for someone's trying to commit the wrong crime at the wrong time.

It was also the kind of baffler that would have drawn Ellery to the point like a setter in the field at the first flutter of a wing. But Ellery had gone back to Turkey.

I'm my son's father, Richard decided with a grimace.

He finished his coffee and prepared a breakfast tray for Jessie, a service she always protested and secretly cherished.

An act of Congress could not have made him return to New York.

"First things first, Jessie," he said.

Jessie looked up from her sausages and eggs. He had bolted the doors, and he was speaking in a voice that would have defied any but the latest electronic bug.

"What things?" Jessie asked.

"We have to start somewhere. And the only fact we have to go on is that you're not the Jessie Sherwood Brass was looking for. So the question has to be answered: How many of the others aren't the genuine article, either? I can't leave you here alone to find out, and even if I could it would take me too long. We need help."

"But who, Richard?"

"My West 87th Street Irregulars," the Inspector said with a grin. "So hold down the fort, will you, honey? I've got to get to that inn again and make some calls."

The great stone fireplace of the Old River Inn had gagged to death long ago, to be replaced by a malodorous oil heater whose fumes pervaded the food, such as it was, and gave the drinks a bouquet of creosote. Otherwise the spready, low-ceilinged dining room was little changed from the days of the Hudson River steamboat trade, when the captains and crews of the *Ben Franklin* and the *Mary Powell* took their pleasure there during layovers. But none of the six men at the scarred and bleached round table in the middle of the dining room was in a mood for nostalgia. The Inspector had insisted on treating his five guests to the grandest feed the Inn afforded, with a bottle of Irish to make it palatable, before getting down to the business for which he had summoned them; and they were plainly chafing for enlightenment.

The old men listened in professional silence as the Inspector outlined the situation at "the bughouse," his least colorful characterization.

They were ex-police officers, retired by the New York City

police department at the mandatory age of sixty-three. Wes Polonsky, a massive man with a mashed nose, had been a detective first grade on the Automobile, Forgery, and Pickpocket Squad. Pete Angelo, Polonsky's old working partner, was even more massive; he had been a terror to hoodlums, and Polonsky, who had been pretty good himself, swore that Angelo could still stack them in a brawl like cordwood. Al Murphy, whose red hair refused to fade, had been a sergeant on radio car patrol in the 16th Precinct at the time of his retirement. Hugh Giffin had come out of the Main Office Squad with a set of broken knuckles and a knife slash across his face; he had a gentle disposition that had never interfered with the heroics sometimes called for by his job. The fifth ex-cop, Johnny Kripps, had been a lieutenant in Homicide. With his black-rimmed glasses and soft white hair he looked like a teacher or librarian.

"What I had in mind," the Inspector said, "is going to call for legwork, maybe a lot of it. None of us is getting any younger—"

"Cut the baloney, Dick," said Pete Angelo. "You wouldn't have thrown us this life preserver if you didn't think we had the muscle to grab it."

"I take real good care of my feet, Inspector," Polonsky said quickly. Of the quintet he seemed the most devastated by time; the hand holding the cigaret shook, and there were red streaks on his eyeballs. "You don't have to worry about us."

The Inspector hesitated. They were all put out to pasture through the cruel chronology of age, when most of them could still run a respectable race; it was about Polonsky that he had his doubts. But to have left out old Wes would have been unthinkable. He made up his mind to give the big Pole the easiest job without making a point of it.

"Wes, you tackle the Alistairs. I'm betting they have more yellow sheets here and yonder than Carter has pills. There's just got to be something on them. Root around the B.C.I., talk to some of the boys, get as much dope as you can dig up. My hunch is they've used aliases all over creation. I figure Alistair for pure con, with that Beast of Belsen wife of his badgering for him. If she is his wife."

"Will do." Old Polonsky's bloodshot eyes were giving off sparks.

"Murph, you tackle this Dr. Thornton. Hubert Thornton, South Cornwall, seems involved in a medical co-op and clinic. Find out especially about his mother, if she ever had a connection with Brass."

Al Murphy reached for the bottle with a red-furred hand.

"I'm great on mother cases," he said with a grin. "I remember one time—"

They hooted him down.

"You, Hughie, draw Cornelia Openshaw," the Inspector said to Giffin. "She's a sex-crazy old maid whose parents are supposed to have saved Brass from committing suicide." He slid over a slip with her address, and the scarred ex-M.O.S. man tucked it away. "I want to know if that story is true."

Angelo was looking expectant. "Okay, Pete, your baby is this young fellow Palmer, Keith Palmer." He handed the big man another slip. "Brass claims Palmer's mother was once a good 'friend' of his. From the way he said it, she shacked up with him when he was something to look at without turning your stomach. It will probably take delicate handling. I don't want word of this to get back to Palmer, so just concentrate on the mother background."

"Leave it to me, Dick."

"Lynn O'Neill is yours, Johnny," the Inspector said to Kripps. "This one may take some doing. The girl is from Wyoming, and her father, the man Brass says saved him from a necktie party, was a sheriff there somewhere. You may even have to fly out."

"Let me give it a long-distance try first," the ex-Homicide lieutenant said. "Just before they put me out to grass I had to pick up an extradited murder suspect at the sheriff's office in Cheyenne, and I got pretty friendly with the chief deputy. I could maybe dig this all up by phone."

"Well, if you can't and you find you have to fly out, Johnny, I'll pick up the tab."

"I wouldn't think of it, Dick." Kripps had turned a brick shade. "Only these days I have to play it close to the vest. . . ."

"It's my case, and I pay the expenses. That goes for the whole crew. Just let me know what you lay out. Or if any of you needs an advance—?"

"What'd you do, Inspector, come into a million?" Polonsky growled. "Look, I'm so damn glad to have something to *do*. . . ."

The rest was friendly argument and what was left of the bottle of Irish. They broke up at last after setting a meeting date at the Inn for progress reports; then Richard Queen went back to The House of Brass feeling far better than when he had left.

4

WHAT!

Lynn O'Neill and Keith Palmer were the only two young people within reaching distance, so they naturally reached.

The atmosphere of the place was no hindrance. There was something about the house and even its tenants that made people uneasy about being left alone. If not for the ever-winking brass, The House of Brass would have had all the hominess of a castle in Transylvania. Lynn especially hated the bedtimes, when she had to lock her door and face the long night in solitary. She could hardly wait for the mornings and the sight of Keith Palmer's rugged and—she was sure of it (or was she?)—decent young face.

"I really don't know what I'm doing here," Lynn confided to Keith on the second morning after the assault on Hendrik Brass. They were strolling through the piny woods behind the outbuildings, Keith kicking fallen branches aside and Lynn picking her way across the ankle-trap terrain; Brass's grounds were as dilapidated as his house. "I ought to go home."

"Oh, I hope you won't do that," Keith said quickly.

"Why not?"

"Because, well, there's all that loot."

"Is that," asked Lynn, sending a sidelong glance his way that sparkled with topaz, "the only reason?"

"Well, no."

"What's another reason?"

"Well, you."

"Oh," Lynn said, and lapsed into encouraging silence.

"I mean, you're a damn attractive wench."

"Oh, dear," Lynn sighed. "I was afraid you were going to say something like that."

"Why afraid?"

"Should I be flattered? Any girl my age would look yummy in this zoo. Who's my competition? Cornelia Openshaw? Not that she wouldn't like to be. The way she looks at you is absolutely pornographic. Or Mrs. Alistair? I imagine it would be like trying to make love to a cougar. Of course, there's that darling Mrs. Queen—"

"Look, it's *you*."

"I don't grasp your meaning, Mr. Palmer."

"I mean," Keith exploded, "you'd stand out in Atlantic City during Miss America week!"

"Why, thank you," murmured Lynn.

"Anyway, what would you do back in Wyoming?"

"Look for another job. They automated me out of my last one."

"You see?"

They zigged along for some time, breathing deeply. In Lynn's case, Keith thought, it was a rousing sight. And a fine day it was. Sun shining, and all that. The farther they got from old Brass's mausoleum the finer the day came, the shinier the sun, and the more energetically Lynn's sweater bounced.

"And another thing," Lynn said suddenly. "It doesn't fit."

"What doesn't fit?"

"Any of this. I'm beginning to feel . . ." Lynn stopped. "Never mind."

"Now you can't do that! What were you going to say?"

"It'll sound square."

"Try me."

"It's . . . evil." Lynn searched his face. But he failed to smile, and she was cheered. "It's not just that eerie old man or his Frankenstein monster. It's nearly all of them—the Alistairs, that Openshaw freak, Mr. Queen always disappearing somewhere. . . . The only ones who give me any feeling of security are Dr. Thornton and Mrs. Queen, and sometimes I'm not sure about them."

"How about me?" Keith asked carelessly.

Lynn squatted on a smooth boulder beside the path. She was wearing blush-pink slacks, and the way they tightened over her flanks when she sat down tickled him.

"How about you, Keith?"

"That was my question."

"Let me ask you a question. I don't have any right to ask it, so you don't have to answer. Are you married?"

Keith was stricken. He stood there.

"I thought so," Lynn said. The sun's rays squeezing through the pines unaccountably dimmed. Lucky Lynn, she thought.

"Now hold on there," Keith stammered. "Just hold your horses. You asked me a question, give me a chance to think how to answer you—"

"Oh, come off it, Keith. How many kinds of answers are there to a question like that? Yes or no, and that's it. Not that it's any of my business, of course."

"I'd *like* it to be your business. I mean—"

"Yes?"

"You asked whether I'm married, and you said there are only two possible answers to it, yes or no. Well, they're not the only possible answers, Lynn. That's what's hanging me up."

"They're not?" Lynn said derisively. "All right, Mr. Palmer, you give me another possible answer."

"Yes *and* no."

Lynn's mouth opened, and she jumped to her feet. "That's the most insulting doubletalk, do you know that? I'm beginning not to like you at all, Keith Palmer!"

"But it's the truth," he protested. He was in the grip of some obscure agony. "In one way I'm married, in another I'm not. I—well, I can't explain it any more definitely than that. Not right now I can't. I mean—"

"You're putting me on. And you needn't bother to see me back to Horror House, thank you. What kind of fool do you take me for?"

Lynn galloped off. He stood there glaring, half hoping she would turn an ankle so that he would have a face-saving excuse to go after her. But she was as agile as a filly. All too soon her nubile young figure was lost among the pines.

Keith Palmer kicked at the boulder. Unfortunately his aim was impeccable. So he sat down cursing his foot, and cursing Keith Palmer and all his works, which included a wife named Joanne and a small boy named Sam, alias Schmulie.

On the fifth night after Hendrik Brass's head's adventure with the fireplace poker, at dinner, Richard Queen rapped on his wineglass, which was still full of Hugo's vile Chablis.

"If you don't mind, Mr. Brass," Richard said, "I'd like everybody to meet in the parlor. Especially including you, sir."

"Oh?" said old Brass. "And if I do mind, Mr. Queen? Aren't you making rather free with my house?"

"Somebody made rather free with your head a few nights ago," the Inspector retorted, "and you didn't seem to mind that, which strikes me as pretty broadminded of you, if you'll pardon the pun. But that's not what's sticking in my craw, Mr. Brass. It's another of your peculiarities, if that's the word."

"And what is that?" asked the old man amiably, as if they were bosom friends. "We can talk here. What's bothering you?"

"What's bothering me, Mr. Brass, and what's going to

bother everybody at this table before I get through, is that you're one of the world's biggest liars."

The Alistairs drew in their heads in tandem, like a brace of trained turtles. They then glanced at each other, whereupon as one they turned their attention to Hendrik Brass. Lynn O'Neill's eyes widened. Keith Palmer's narrowed. Dr. Thornton's reflected the watchfulness with which he seemed increasingly infected. Only Cornelia Openshaw remained unmoved. She was digesting young Palmer from across the table, what could be seen of him, piece by piece.

"I'm a liar?" old Brass said calmly. "Indeed. And wherein have I lied?"

"You said that Jessie Sherwood's father, Dr. Sherwood, once saved your life when you were very sick. Isn't that what you said?"

"It's exactly what I said."

"Well, far from saving your life, Dr. Sherwood nearly killed you. He made a wrong diagnosis and prescribed a treatment from which you almost died. If a specialist hadn't been called and corrected both the diagnosis and the treatment, you *would* have died. When you recovered, you went to a lawyer and actually started to sue Dr. Sherwood for malpractice. Only the fact that the specialist wouldn't testify against a fellow-physician made you drop the suit. And that's how grateful you had reason to be to Dr. Sherwood!"

"I see," said Hendrik Brass, and he hawked. "I see," he said again, and he smiled. "Is that all, Mr. Queen?"

"I'm just starting. Take DeWitt Alistair's father." Alistair's floridity lost some of its bloom; but Elizabeth Alistair contrived to gather herself in an almost visible ripple of muscle. "One time, you said, when you were hard-pressed financially and couldn't find a soul to help you out, Alistair's father lent you what you needed to save you from bankruptcy. Didn't you get it hindside to, Mr. Brass? Alistair's father didn't come to your rescue. He didn't lend you a cent. What really happened was that you owed him a big gambling debt, and he made your life miserable trying to get you to pay up. It was his demands for payment, in fact, that almost drove you *into* bankruptcy. That's what Alistair's father did for you that, according to you, Mr. Brass, brings a lump to your throat at his memory."

It was an index of DeWitt Alistair's need for some providential black-ink bookkeeping that he directed the full volume of his malevolence, not at Hendrik Brass, but at the Inspector. But Richard Queen had been audited by such glances before, and he ignored it. As for Elizabeth Alistair, she lidded her stony eyes like an Internal Revenue inspector.

"Go on," said Brass. "Because I take it you're not through?"

The Inspector looked around as if for refreshment and settled on Lynn's lovely face. "Miss O'Neill is another victim of your lying. Her father didn't save you from a lynching. And he didn't come to your defense at your trial. He caught you redhanded with the stolen horse and was the prosecution's most important witness against you. The only reason you didn't wind up in jail is that he committed a technical error—search and seizure without a warrant—and the presiding judge happened to be a stickler for the fine points. If you've got any reason to remember somebody with gratitude, it's the judge, not Sheriff O'Neill. He felt so bad about your getting off that he ran you out of his county, threatening to string you up himself if ever he caught you horse-thieving again."

Hendrik Brass's long neck stretched; he ran out his gray tongue and made a hissing noise. Then it all turned to cackles.

"You've been doing a lot of homework, Mr. Queen. There's more?"

"Oh, yes," the Inspector said, turning from Lynn, who was trying not to make a spectacle of herself. Her expression said: There goes my million. "Let's go to Keith Palmer here. You said that you and Palmer's mother were very close. You know how close your mother was to this man?" he said to Keith. "She couldn't stand the sight of him. She queered his act with her best friend, whom he was trying to marry, by proving to the girl that Brass was a skunk who'd left a trail of broken hearts, and that the only reason he was after her was to get his hands on her father's money. And he has the gall to imply that he and your mother had an affair!"

"Is that true, Mr. Brass?" Keith asked the old man. "For God's sake, why would you make up a story like that?"

"Mr. Queen has the floor," Hendrik Brass said, unveiling his dentures. "Let him answer your questions."

"Next case," the Inspector said, unveiling *his* dentures. "That's you, Dr. Thornton. Whose mother is supposed to have hauled him to his feet at a low point in his life, and restored his confidence in himself, I believe he put it. Doctor, your mother had about as much use for this man as Palmer's did. He tried to get her to marry him, and put on a campaign of harassment that lasted six months—one time she had to call the police to get him out of her hair. She finally shook him when she married your father, and even then your father had to threaten to break his neck if he didn't leave your mother alone."

Dr. Thornton seemed unsurprised. He examined Brass through his heavy glasses as if the old man were a specimen under his microscope.

Brass was silent this time. He merely waved his gray hand at the Inspector. The crooked smile was still in evidence.

"Which brings me," the Inspector said, "to Miss Openshaw—"

"Stop! I don't want to hear it!" cried Cornelia Openshaw; she was completely engaged by now, Keith Palmer forgotten. She actually stopped up her ears.

"Sorry, you're part of this, Miss Openshaw, and in fairness to the others I can't leave you out. In your case the finding is negative. Brass claims your parents saved his life when he tried to commit suicide. There's not a record or a recollection on the part of anyone in a position to know that it was true. In view of what we've learned about the parents of the others, it makes more sense to assume that, whatever relationship your father and mother had with this man, it left him not with gratitude toward them but with some gripe he's nursed for a generation."

"You can't prove that," snapped the spinster. "I for one am ready to believe anything Mr. Brass says."

"That's your problem. Well, Brass? That's the record. Want to correct it?"

"So that's why you've been making all those trips to the Old River Inn," the old man tittered. "Hugo wondered about that, and so did I."

"Look, Brass, you've been caught dead to rights in at least five whoppers, and the time's come for you to start leveling. All these people's parents are dead, so you can't take anything out on them. But they left children. If you're the sort of man who carries over his hates, you hate them. Then why have you invited them here? To make them your heirs, as you claim? After what I've dug up about you, nobody in his right mind would believe it. And there's at least one of these people who didn't from the start—the one who tried to wallop your brains out. If you ask me, he thought he was beating you to the punch! So what's this all about, Brass? Did you get them here so you could have Hugo dose the lousy food he serves with arsenic? From the samples of his cooking, we wouldn't be able to taste the difference. Come clean!"

Old Brass, who had been nestled in the recesses of his big chair at the head of the table, inched forward and up until he was perched on the edge, the whole process recalling a horror movie in which the 3000-year-old mummy suddenly sits up in his sarcophagus.

"Hugo," he said briskly, "more coffee."

Hugo jerked, shambled forward with the coffeepot, and refilled the old man's cup. He remained behind the chair, pot aloft, electric cord trailing, so that he looked like a plugged-in robot.

"Ah." Brass set the cup deftly down on the saucer. "You were asking me a question, Mr. Queen, and you've earned an answer. All that running about between here and the inn, meeting with your hirelings—if that's what they are—getting their reports and so on—a bunch of incompetents, if you ask me, because they got everything right but the only thing that counts."

"What are you talking about?" The Inspector looked startled. "What didn't they get right?"

"Why, they dug up the facts," sniggered Hendrik Brass, "about the wrong Hendrik Brass."

The snigger became a laugh that became a spasm that left the old man choking. He was slapping his skeletal shank with the marvelous humor of it all and trying to get his breath at the same time. There was rack-brained silence around the board until he achieved it, and after.

"What d'ye mean the wrong Hendrik Brass?" Richard Queen roared. "Make sense, man. There's more than one Hendrik Brass—that's your story? You'll have to do better than that!"

"It's easy enough to check," Brass gasped; and to the Inspector's disgust one of the birchbark lids came down over its sightless eye in a wink. "But you'll find out I'm not lying. There's been more Hendrik Brasses than you can count. It's a family tradition?"

"*What's* a family tradition?"

"Two traditions. One: The family business has always been inherited by the eldest son. Any other sons take potluck. Two: The eldest son is always named Hendrik, after the founder of the Brass fortune. My father had two sons. I was the younger. My elder brother was baptized Hendrik Willem—sometimes the eldest was given a middle name; optional, you might say. But always Hendrik. When I came along I was named Simon."

"Then why are you calling yourself Hendrik?"

"Because Henk is dead—I used to call Hendrik Henk. That left only me, you see. So I had a lawyer apply to the court to change my name legally to Hendrik Simon Brass. It's been Hendrik Simon ever since."

"Hold on! Are you saying that the Hendrik I've been talking about, the one who bedeviled the parents of these people, was your older brother?"

"I am." The old man grinned his grisly grin. "And a wild one he was, too, in his young days, when Father was still alive and running the business. Almost as wild as I was. Got around the country quite a bit, Hendrik Willem did. But when Father died, Henk came home and settled down. Turned out a regular jackass for work, like Father. Work, work, work, that was Henk. Didn't even take time enough off to get married, though he'd doodled around with women a-plenty in his early days. And one fine day Henk dropped dead from plain overwork, and the business and the money and this property fell into my lap. And here we are. Does that satisfy you, Mr. Queen?"

The Inspector glared at him. There had been no reason for Polonsky, Angelo, Murphy, Giffin, and Kripps to suspect a different Hendrik Brass; it was the last thing anyone would have thought of. Still . . .

"You haven't straightened this out at all, Mr. Brass. It's crooked as my Aunt Minnie's arthritis—crookeder! Your brother did all those things? But you led us to believe *you* did. The identical involvements couldn't apply to both of you, even if you both raised hell as young men. *Two* near fatal mistakes by the same doctor, one involving you and one your brother? *Two* arrests for horse-stealing by the same Wyoming sheriff of the same brothers at different times? And so on? That would be a fairy tale, Brass. Or are you trying to make us believe that the stories you told us about the nice things those folks did were things done to you, but the stuff my friends dug out about the nasty things they did were things done to your brother? The same people? That would be an even taller story!

"The way I see it, Brass, you personally had no contact at all with the parents of these people here. That being the case, you personally can't possibly owe them a thing—not gratitude, not even hate. Or are you carrying on a feud in your brother's name?"

"That," old Brass chuckled, "is for you to find out."

"Well, I don't buy such a fairy tale, either. Feuds went out with the Hatfields and the Whatchamacallems. You've got some other reason, Brass. Why did you ask these folks to come here? It still gets down to the same thing: What's this all about?"

"Yes, that seems to be the six-million-dollar question, doesn't it, Inspector?" said the old man with gummy enjoyment. "Oh, dear, I let the cat out of the bag, didn't I? I don't suppose anybody here but your wife knows. You didn't know I knew you were a retired police inspector from New York, did you?"

"No," said the Inspector with something like respect, "I did not."

Which made them all stare at him, emphatically the Alistairs, who looked as if they had just turned over a rock with the usual unpleasant results.

"I may be blind," chortled old Brass, "but there's nothing wrong with my head, hey? Or with my sources of information? All right, Inspector Queen, you've had considerable experience solving mysteries, suppose you solve this one. *You* find out what this is all about, eh? What say?" And all of a sudden his merriment drained out. He grimaced, and stamped his foot, and yelped, "I've had enough fun for one night. Hugo, you barrel of fish guts, my cane!"

5

WHICH?

Hendrik Brass's "sources of information" turned up the next morning, in the singular.

It happened while Dr. Thornton was attempting to dress the old man's head in the brassy bedroom. Jessie was there to assist, Richard Queen was there because Jessie was there, and Hugo was there because of Richard's standing order—humped in a corner not being used for the moment, flawed eyes trained on the bandages swathing the aged skull across the room as if they were about to reveal something rare and wonderful.

Dr. Thornton said, "Peroxide, please," and Nurse Queen obliged, and the doctor poured, soaking the old bandage above the wound. He waited while the peroxide bubbled and the caked blood underneath softened, and then gently unwound the bandage, Hendrik Brass lying there after his fit of temper with a mummified expression, sunken eyes shut; at the last deft pull the dressing came away like a charm, the eyes opened, and the old man said suddenly to his ceiling, "You have healing hands, Doctor."

"Thank you," Dr. Thornton said. " 'I dressed his wounds; God healed them.' "

The ancient imp looked puzzled.

"What?"

"Something I read somewhere."

"God! I don't believe in God."

The wound was ugly. There was a marked swelling along the puckered line of laceration, tightening the stitches so that the bald skull looked like a football with its laces showing.

"I don't think we'll rebandage," the doctor said. "Let the air get at it. I'll remove the stitches in a day or two. Right now we'll clean away the mess. Have you been having any headaches or head pains? Dizziness? Faintness?"

"No."

"The God you don't believe in has been good to you, Mr. Brass."

He and Jessie got busy with the clotted blood around the wound, Richard admiring his wife's smooth movements; so that he was startled at the sound of Hugo's voice.

"The man is here, the man is here!"

To the Inspector's ears as he whirled it might as well have been "I smell the blood of an Englishman!", in so ferocious a bass had Hugo uttered it. And then he saw the man.

He stood lounging in the doorway, hands in pockets, with a smile that was half jeer, half sneer, and all of it nasty. It was hard to tell exactly what amused him, whether it was Hugo's mastiff growl, the Inspector's choreography, or the wound on Brass's skull.

Hugo took a step.

"Watch it, Shorty," the man in the doorway said. "I may not be as big as you, but I'm betting I'm a lot quicker on my pins. Not to mention hands."

Hugo took another step. The newcomer did not move, either forward or backward. But the Inspector saw him set himself.

"He doesn't like me," the man said. "I don't think we'll ever make the scene."

"Who are you?" Richard demanded.

"The name, dad, is Vaughn." He kept his eyes on Hugo.

"Who, who?" shrilled old Hendrik from the bed. "Vaughn?"

"That's right, Mr. Brass."

"Hugo," the old man said peevishly. "I told you the last time. Stop."

Hugo stopped. The man uncoiled and advanced at a saunter into the bedroom.

The Inspector was a peaceable citizen, but there was something about the newcomer that made him itch to push the fellow's face in. For one thing, his very walk was an affront—a cross between a slither and a strut, engineered either to pounce or to strike an attitude, depending on circumstances. For another, his survey of Jessie was a laser performance, penetrating deep; it stripped her quite naked and, worse, discarded her in a sort of regretful contempt; he might just as well have said aloud: Twenty years ago, baby . . . maybe.

You and I, the Inspector told him silently, were born enemies.

He took a survey of his own.

Either Vaughn's custom pinstripe was made too small for him, or he had grown too broad and thick for it; it revealed rather than covered his body, which looked overmuscled. His hair was stiff and sandy and cropped short. His light gray eyes had diamond-chip glints in them. His nose was flattened in an otherwise angular face; perhaps it was the jaw that made the Inspector think of a cartoon, for it jutted out of his face like a 1925 cowcatcher. His skin was pitted and unlovely and shrieked of sunlamps. The Inspector would not have been surprised to see him produce a racing form and a slice of Lindy's cheesecake. There was a Bersagliere-type hat on his head (he's a sharpshooter, all right, the Inspector thought); he had not bothered to remove it. His shirt was navy blue and his tie was daffodil yellow. The hands were big and scarred. Yet there was intelligence in the spying eyes; or perhaps a primitive wisdom that had been picked up in back rooms and alleys. It was impossbile to imagine a decent man liking him or a woman of any sort turning her head away.

Anyway you looked at him, he was bad news.

"What happened to your noggin?" Vaughn asked with the passion of a coroner.

The old man said petulantly, "I will discuss that with you later, Mr. Vaughn."

"You should have contacted me. That overgrown slob is no security. Even a blind man ought to be able to see he's got nothing between his cauliflowers but air."

"You," Jessie said, "are a boor!"

"Sure, doll," Vaughn said, and dismissed her.

"Please, please," the old man said. "The rest of you get out."

"Hold it." The Inspector's mustache was bristling. "My wife, not to mention the others, has a vested interest in what goes on in this house. I want to know who this man is and why you've had him come here."

"You make like a cop," Vaughn said before Brass could answer. "Say, I catch. Your name is Queen and you just got tied to Jessie Sherwood—I take it this broad here. Right, dad?"

"You're right, sonny, and nobody calls my wife a broad. *Nobody!*"

"Pops, you turn me on." The way the muscular back presented itself to him made the Inspector angry indeed. But Jessie put her hand on his arm. "You. With the lip rug. Which one would you be?"

The doctor's red mustache bristled, too. "I'm Dr. Thornton."

"Oh, yeah. Okay, you heard Mr. Brass. Out, the lot of you."

"I'm not leaving this room till I've had my answer," the Inspector said. "Who is this hood, Mr. Brass?"

"It's all right, Vaughn," Hendrik Brass said. "On second thought I want them to know. Why, Inspector, Mr. Vaughn is the private detective I engaged to find your wife and the others. He is also an attorney. He will draw up my will when I've made up my mind who gets my money."

"Attorney! Which school did you graduate from, Vaughn? Ossining?"

"Harvard, Yale, Barbers' College, what's the big deal? You want to see my degree, dad?"

"I'd like to see the permit for that gun you're packing in the shoulder holster."

"And I thought this three-hundred-buck custom-built hid the heater. I better change tailors. Don't fret your old gray head, Inspector. I've got a permit. Also, if you're interested, a New York detective agency license."

"They're letting anything operate in New York these days. All right, Mr. Brass, he's your one-man Gestapo, and I can't do anything about that, but I want it understood now that he'd better not try any rough stuff. Especially with the women. I know the breed."

Vaughn shrugged. "What's the matter, granddad, aren't the wedding bells swinging anymore? Look, if it's like war you want, okay, only I choose my own turf. And just so we understand each other, watch that fat lip. An ex-cop is nothing by me." He gave the Inspector no time to reply. "How long's this job going to take, Mr. Brass?"

"As long as it takes." The old man looked sly. "How long can you be away from your place of business?"

"That's up to you, you're picking up the tab. While we're holding hands—and since I have to hang around here anyway—you're not serious about letting Man Mountain there keep muscling for you, are you? If that hit on your skull says anything about his work, you better get yourself a new boy."

"That's what I had in mind, Mr. Vaughn. You're also to take over as my bodyguard."

Hugo stirred. "Not me?" He looked appalled.

"Beat it, Godzilly," Vaughn said. "You heard your lord and master."

"Not me?" Hugo said again; this time it sounded like a whimper.

"No," the old man yapped. "You go back to your polishing, Hugo. And be sure and do whatever Mr. Vaughn tells you. Hear?"

Hugo's shoulders sloped. "Yes, Mr. Hendrik." He slunk from the room. Jessie could have wept for him.

"All right, folks, Outsville time." Vaughn jerked a hammerhead thumb toward the door. "Mr. Brass and I have some yakking to do."

Richard held the door open for Jessie and a fuming Dr. Thornton. He was about to follow them out when, to his stupefaction, he saw Vaughn reach, produce a battered silver flask from his hip pocket, and unscrew the cap. The last time had had seen anyone carrying a hip flask was during Prohibition. Maybe they were coming back. Or Vaughn had been reading Dashiell Hammett. If he could read.

The last thing the Inspector saw as he closed the door was Vaughn taking a long pull from the flask.

"Great spot you've got here, Mr. Brass," he heard the private eye laugh. "But like I say, it'll never take the place of Acapulco."

Before Vaughn's coming, life in the old house had settled into a restless routine: breakfast between eight and nine; drives into Phillipskill or Tarrytown for newspapers, magazines, books (the Brass library, such as it was, had apparently stopped growing in the time of William Dean Howells and F. Marion Crawford), cigarets or toiletries; then lunch at noon, after which some strolled about the grounds or down to the half-submerged boat landing, or occupied themselves in other ways—Jessie knitting a pullover for Richard with needles and yarn she bought in the Phillipskill Emporium; the Alistairs playing poker for toothpicks, or Mrs. Alistair engaging herself in a carnivorous solitaire while her husband pored over his racing news, purchased in Tarrytown; Dr. Thornton reading the latest issue of *Playboy*, ignoring the copies of the AMA journal and *MD* which had been forwarded to him from South Cornwall; the two young people reading paperbacks, ostentatiously avoiding each other in all but spirit, Lynn giving Keith the nose-in-the-air bit signifying outrage, Keith taking it like a superfluous puppy and looking so miserable that Lynn wanted to put her arms around him and assure him that everything was all right, which was ridiculous, since everything was all wrong; Cornelia Openshaw roasting Keith with her superheated glances while her posture and behavior spoke of absolute propriety; and over all old fox Queen, here and everywhere, but never far from their host who mingled with his guests, present but aloof, pale ears cocked for nuances, like an old conductor listening to a new orchestra, with a smile on his lips that positively smoked, it was so infernal. It made peace of mind and dreams of millions difficult. But even this became routine, and after a while most of them ignored Hendrik Brass except when directly addressed, at which times they leaped to his question or bidding, smiling anxious smiles in return, as if he could see.

Vaughn's appearance on the premises changed the quality of their discomfort. It was like being enclosed suddenly in a huge spherical sneer from which there was no escape.

Like the Inspector, Vaughn had apparently taken the measure of the Alistairs; he kept delivering little seminars on confidence games he had run into, and pretending forgetfulness of the fine points and appealing to them for help. It unsettled the pair wonderfully, since Vaughn deferred to their expertise within hearing of old Brass, who listened in enigmatic silence.

On Dr. Thornton he spewed the venom of an evident animus against the medical profession. All doctors, he would remark, were butchers, money grubbers, or out-and-out quacks. The doctor suffered with dignity. But equanimity grew harder for him by the hour, especially when Vaughn took to making gentle duck sounds at his approach. Thornton began to tug at his mustache, show his tobacco-stained teeth, and make fists. Yet Vaughn always stopped short of lighting Thornton's fuse. Apparently it was a way of amusing himself.

His technique with Cornelia Openshaw was basic: he told her dirty stories. In the beginning this sent her stalking out of the room, or drove her into incoherent splutters. But the Inspector noticed that Miss Openshaw's indignation threshold became higher as time passed, until finally she stopped stalking and spluttering, and listened in a simulation of total deafness.

Toward Palmer Vaughn adopted the man-to-man ploy. It consisted of little unexpected jabs to the ribs, like punctuation marks: "Y'know what I mean, man"—*jab* exclamation point; or a powerful slap between the shoulder blades that rocked Keith, big as he was: "What d'ye say, pal—*slap* question mark; or a hard forefinger stabbing at Keith's chest like a row of hemstitching: "You can bet your sweet asafetida, fella"—*stab-stab-stab* period . . . always uttered and delivered in the friendliest fashion, so that it would have seemed churlish to take umbrage. The procedure consistently reduced Keith to speechlessness. After a while it was embarrassing to see Keith backpedal or sidestep at the approach of Vaughn, like an outclassed fighter suddenly thrust into the ring. It was a question how long he would take Vaughn's badgering.

But it was Lynn O'Neill who became Vaughn's serious target. His technique was to pretend not to see her until she came close; then to start with pleased surprise; then to begin at the crown of her chestnut hair and go over her slowly from north to south like a photoelectric eye searching for hidden treasures, lingering on those he found, until he reached her feet, when he reversed his field and repeated the process from south to north. He said hardly a word to her; his eyes spoke for him. Since his only passes were ocular, Lynn could find no graceful way to slap him down. She developed a chronic blush, which infuriated her, and fled as soon as she could.

"The poor girl," Jessie said indignantly. Said Richard, "He's softening her up." "What do you *mean*?" "It takes a powerful gal to resist such flattery." "Flattery!" "To her sex appeal. Do you see Keith Palmer getting anywhere with his droopy looks? A woman likes a man who wants her, doesn't she?" "Not a man like *that*!" "You couldn't be wronger," Richard said; and there developed between the newlyweds a certain coolness that lasted the better part of a morning.

Richard had to admit that, as far as Vaughn's day-to-day assignment was concerned, his work could not be faulted. During the day he was rarely beyond arm's length of Hendrik; and when the old man went to his room for the night, Vaughn set up a cot in the hall straddling the doorway. If a door was opened anywhere, or a footfall or a voice got to his ears, he was out of the cot like a shot, hand darting to his holster, either to investigate or to wait where he was until he was satisfied that the sound augured no threat to his charge. He bathed and changed his clothes in the afternoons in Brass's bedroom, when the blind man took his daily nap, and then only after latching and locking the bedroom door.

There were no incidents, only a clotting of relationships. The Alistairs remained a duo, rarely separating—once Alistair drove down to the Old River Inn to make a telephone call, he said, and his wife paced the parlor until he returned; after dinner they usually played cards, ignoring the others. Hendrik Brass and Vaughn formed another set, with Hugo lumbering dumbly along on their periphery. The others, with the indecisive exception of Cornelia Openshaw, constituted the largest clique; Miss Openshaw could not seem to make up her mind between the Brass-Vaughn-Hugo group or the one that included young Palmer. She flitted from one to the other like a disoriented bee.

One night after dinner the spinster wandered over to the ancient cabinet Zenith and began to play with the dials. Nothing happened, which was not surprising, since the Inspector had seen her go through the same routine at least twice before. "Goodness, not even the radio works," Miss Openshaw said. "Mr. Palmer, would you mind driving me over to the Inn? They have a TV there."

She was obviously on the prowl. Keith flushed.

"I'd like to, Miss Openshaw, but Miss O'Neill and I have a date to go walking. Don't we, Lynn?"

He fully expected to be thrown to the wolverine. Instead, Lynn said, "Of course, Keith. I'm sorry, Miss Openshaw. I'm sure Mr. Palmer will be happy to oblige some other night. Coming, Keith?"

Outside, Keith, hustling Lynn along, blurted, "Thanks a million. It was the only thing I could think of."

Lynn giggled. "She really has a thing for you."

"That's the way it's been all my life. The ones I go for won't give me the time of night. The ones that go for me are dogs."

"Oh, I'm sure that's not true. Didn't you say something about being married—in a way? Whatever that meant. Or did you marry a dog?—what a nasty word!"

"No! I mean . . . Look, Lynn," Keith said, "about this marriage business . . . Oh, damn it, I simply can't explain! I mean, all I can say is I'm not a two-timer. It's not my nature. Lynn, trust me. I want to get to know you—"

"Why?" Lynn said remotely . . . not quite as remotely as during their last walk, but remotely enough to let him know she wasn't to be taken in by a lot of sweet talk from a married man on the make.

"Because—Hell! Why does a man usually want to get to know a girl?"

"Do you really want me to answer that?"

"Well, of course that becomes part of it—"

"Of *course*."

"But not the whole part, or even the most important part—"

"Oh, I don't know," Lynn said. "It's pretty important. Anyway, let's drop the subject and enjoy the woods. Lovely country, isn't it? So different from Wyoming."

They exchanged biographies, feeling better. Lynn's original family home had been in a coal-mining town which went ghost after the veins ran out. "Easterners have an idea everybody from the West is a cowhand. Wyoming has more sheep than cattle, and darn few of either where I grew up. Daddy died when I was thirteen and my mother went a few years ago. I could certainly use that million dollars. I don't even have a job."

"You," Keith said warmly, "could get a job in Hollywood, and not processing food, either."

"*Mister* Palmer. That's one of the oldest lines there is," Lynn said in a weary-wise tone. Secretly she was pleased; he had said it almost as if he meant it—well, really as if he *had* meant it. "And what's your tale of woe?"

He seemed to brace himself, and spun an abbreviated account of his partnership in a junk and scrap iron business "with a marvelous guy named Bill Perlberg"; then of Vietnam and the Saigon bars and the wily Cong, and so on; and in none of it appeared the names Joanne and little Sam, or even the words wife and son, which might have explained the abbreviation, but of course Lynn didn't know that, although she suspected all sorts of things. As for Keith, he tried to change the subject.

Lynn listened critically, walking in judgment, and decided to let him have it. "You're leaving things out," she said, as Zola might have said, *"J'accuse!"* "Why, Keith?"

He was saved by a fluty soprano tootling, "Oh, Mr. Palllllmer! Mr. Palmer?" Or was he? For it was Miss Openshaw, skittering. "Oh, there you are! It's really Miss O'Neill I'm looking for."

"Me?" Lynn said.

"Mrs. Queen wants you. Right away."

"I'll take you back, Lynn," Keith said in a rush.

"No, Mr. Palmer, Mrs. Queen doesn't want *you*. Why don't I keep you company until Miss O'Neill gets back? Miss O'Neill, Mrs. Queen is *waiting*"—and she gave Lynn a friendly shove, and at once latched onto Keith's arm—"oh, I'm so glad to get out of that *house*, Mr. Palmer. That old man gives me the jeebies. Do you know I sometimes get the feeling that he's *looking* at me? I know that awful creature Vaughn definitely is. . . ."

Lynn had to suffer Vaughn's examination as she passed him taking Hendrik up to bed from the parlor. This time something was added. He brushed against her, and his big hand somehow made contact with her bottom. She was about to whirl on him when he said politely, "Pardon *me*, Miss O'Neill," and went on up the stairs. His back laughed at her.

Lynn strode indignantly into the parlor. "Miss Openshaw says you want to see me, Mrs. Queen."

Jessie was knitting; the Inspector was reading yesterday's New York *Daily News*. They both looked up.

"Well, I'm always glad to see you, dear," Jessie said in a puzzled way. "But—"

"What my wife means, Miss O'Neill," the Inspector said with a grin, "is that she was wondering out loud if everybody wouldn't like some tea, and she happened to mention that she didn't see you here. That was all the excuse Miss Openshaw needed. Before anybody could say 'Keith Palmer!' she lit out."

Lynn said rather carefully, "She's pathetic."

"But persistent," Dr. Thornton snapped. He was reading a learned piece by Hugh Hefner angrily. "My advice, Miss O'Neill, is not to waste your sympathy on her. Women of her sort can become dangerous. If I were you, I'd tell Palmer to stay out of her way."

Lynn shrugged. "He's a big boy, Doctor, and I hardly know him. Oh, dear, I'm getting a headache. I think I'll go to bed."

"Four aces," DeWitt Alistair said to his wife, and reached for a mountain of toothpicks.

That was the night the Inspector decided to check with his Irregulars on their last assignment. It was taking too much time, and his nose told him that time was growing short.

"You should have been chairman of the board, Inspector Queen," old Brass said with his gummy grin. "What's the purpose of this conference?"

He was perched on the edge of his paterfamilias chair like some Lilliputian monarch, sucking on the handle of his cane, the lights bouncing off the brass onto his bald head with its football lacing. Vaughn and Hugo flanked him. There was a full audience. For once they were more interested in the Inspector than in their benefactor; there had been something in the Queen voice when he sounded the tocsin that rang through the musty house like the last trump.

"I'll make it short, Mr. Brass," the Inspector said. "You got all these people here on the yarn that you're worth six million dollars—"

"Yarn?" the old man interrupted. He was sucking, twitching, cocking his ears with every appearance of anticipation.

"Yarn," the Inspector repeated. "Because I've had my investigators checking for ten days. In Phillipskill. In Tarrytown. All over Westchester County. In New York. In Boston and Philadelphia, where there's a lot of Back Bay and Main Line money deposited and invested. In New York, Boston, and Philly I set a reliable agency to work on it. What I wanted was quick but thorough coverage, and my crew couldn't do it all themselves. And what they've come up with is this."

Something like horror had leaped into every eye.

"My people haven't been able to find a single checking or savings account or safe deposit box anywhere in the name of Hendrik Brass. Or any record of stocks or bonds, or of financial holdings of any kind. They've found no trace of real estate except this house and the grounds. The house is rated a white elephant by the local real estate people, and the land is worth just about the amount of the outstanding mortgages, of which there are two. In other words, there's practically no equity in your House of Brass."

"Indeed," the old man said with enjoyment. "Your wife isn't the only one who's been doing her knitting, I see."

"I'm not through knitting yet," the Inspector retorted. "My people also turned up the fact that you're over your head in debt to tradespeople in Phillipskill and Tarrytown. The butchers and grocers are carrying you with at least six months' bills. You haven't settled your last winter's fuel bills and come next winter, as I understand it, you'll either pay up or you'll have to go back to heating this antique the way your ancestors did. You're in your third month of arrears to the power company, and one of these days, unless you clear the account, they're going to shut off your service. And the reason you don't like telephones is that the phone company did cut off your service eight months ago for nonpayment. So how many millions can you have, Mr. Brass? And where are they? The way it looks now, the only estate anybody can inherit is a bunch of IOUs."

His audience looked as if he had just announced that they had been enjoying the hospitality of Typhoid Mary.

"Well, Mr. Brass?"

"About the unpaid bills," the old man replied calmly. "Why should I hurry? Yes, some of them are becoming impatient, but let 'em. They'll get over it. Didn't you know they'd rather have a rich man owe them than a poor man pay?—because they can keep adding interest to the bills. As for the telephone company, who needs a telephone? I paid their damned fixed charges for years, and for what? Ninety percent of the calls people make are a waste of time, anyway—jaw-jaw-jaw. Does that answer your question, Inspector?"

"It wouldn't satisfy a two-year-old. But the money you owe is the least of it. How about the money you're supposed to have? You haven't answered that."

The withered mouth parted, and the old man had to make a grab for his false teeth. He seemed delighted with himself;

worse, with Richard Queen, as if the Inspector, like a small boy, had run to him with some treasure of the field to admire. The falsetto of his amusement filled the flickering parlor and its dusty furniture and ricocheted off the time-cracked portraits of the he-Brasses in their stocks and the she-Brasses in their crinolines. They could only gape at him as if he were about to announce that he was the Wizard of Oz.

Hendrik Brass wiped his sightless eyes with a frayed handkerchief.

"You've made me very happy, Inspector Queen." But his voice was now shrewd and cruel. "I'm glad you've snooped. It gives our little game a zing—you know? Think you've caught the old scamp, hey? Well, that's as it may be. I leave it to these good people to decide. Whom will you believe, ladies and gentlemen? This man, who claims I'm a lying pauper, or me? Think it over, my friends. Make up your minds whether I'm penniless, in which case you can leave my house tomorrow morning—with the missing halves of the thousand dollar bills, as I promised—or whether I'm a millionaire and stay. It's up to you." He rose and said peremptorily, "Dummy, your arm! Vaughn, come."

"Daddyo," Vaughn said with admiration, "you blow my cool!"

Silence followed the trio out of the parlor and up the stairs and beyond. It was a long time before it was broken.

Then the Inspector said, "As the old filbert says, it's up to you."

Dr. Thornton had been shaking his head. "I don't know," he said. "I just don't know whether to stay or go."

"What do you think we ought to do, Inspector?" Cornelia Openshaw asked anxiously. "What are you going to advise your wife?"

"Me? I wouldn't leave for ten times the millions he's dangling in front of your noses."

"But I thought you said—"

"Something's going on that isn't right, Miss Openshaw, and I'm staying till I find out what it is."

"Well." Miss Openshaw seemed in agony.

Lynn O'Neill was tossing her chestnut locks. "I simply don't know what we're panicking for. Inspector Queen and his friends can't possibly have covered every place. Mr. Brass could still have his millions on deposit or invested somewhere. I've read that lots of rich people have their money banked in Switzerland, or somewhere else abroad. I'd stay if I were you, Doctor. Think how you'd feel if you found you'd walked out on a million dollars."

"That's his bait," Thornton muttered. "But I do admit that if there is a fortune . . . With a million I could enlarge our clinic, buy the latest equipment, expand our services. . . . I suppose I'll stay. How about you, Keith?"

Young Palmer grinned. "A fire and flood couldn't drive me away. I don't care what you found or didn't find, Inspector. The way I look at it, he's playing poker with us. You don't get up and walk away from a pot like this."

"Even" asked the Inspector dryly, "if you suspect you're playing with a stacked deck?"

"All my chips consist of is time. And I've got plenty of that."

The Inspector was heard to mumble something about P. T. Barnum and the birthrate of suckers, but only by his wife.

"He could have hidden assets," Jessie said suddenly. "All this brass, for instance."

"Why, that's *true,*" Cornelia squealed. "And none of us saw it but Mrs. Queen. The brass must be worth a fortune!"

"You said you'd been in the scrap metal business, Keith," Lynn cried. "Do you know anything about brass?"

"Some." Keith picked up the wicker basket with its brass casing and went over it carefully. Then he examined one of the brass lamps, hefting it repeatedly. Then he examined a late Dutch trundle bed in the same fashion—it had been plated with the omnipresent brass and converted into a magazine rack. He shook his head. "In my opinion all this stuff is ordinary brass of average composition, weight, and workmanship. Maybe below average."

"Even so," Dr. Thornton protested, "there must be tons of it lying around here."

Keith shook his head. "I don't think you could figure the total value in more than thousands. What could you do with sub-par brass in all sizes and shapes but strip it and have it melted down to scrap?"

"Well, I still think we oughtn't to give up hope," Cornelia declared. "Mr. Brass did send us those bills, and if he's a pauper where did he get them? Didn't you say they're genuine, Inspector Queen?"

"The ones my wife got are."

"There, you see?"

The Inspector shrugged.

"Just—one—minute." Lynn was looking around. "This house if full of antiques. Some of them are probably rare."

"Whatever he's got that was worth anything, Miss O'Neill, he's spoiled by plating it with this brass. Anyway, it's all falling apart."

Silence.

"Say!" Keith exclaimed. "The House of Brass used to deal in precious stones, too, didn't it? Why can't his millions be in jewels? Diamonds and stuff wouldn't take up much space if you wanted to hide them. They could be under our noses!"

"It's possible." The Inspector did not sound excited. "The only ones," he went on slowly, "who haven't expressed an opinion are you people." He was staring at the Alistairs. "What are you intending to do? You staying or leaving?"

DeWitt Alistair opened his mouth.

"Staying," his wife said, and took a fortune in toothpicks with a straight flush.

A day passed, and another. Keith and Lynn, spelunking in the cavernous cellar, which was full of fat spiders, broken furniture, and shelving loaded with old kerosene lamps, corroded pipe fittings, empty wine bottles, boxes of rusted nails and screws, and other junk—apparently Hendrik Brass never threw out anything—found no treasure but a mildewed phonograph cabinet and a boxful of ancient records, some of them in undamaged condition. The phonograph was one of the early massive Victrolas, wound by hand, and many of the records were thick platters with Red Seal labels and blank backs—Carusos, Melbas, Schumann-Heinks, Louise Homers, Geraldine Farrars, Titta Ruffos, Mary Gardens, Alma Glucks—some departed Brass had evidently been fond of opera—and a selection of popular recordings of a simpler day.

They lugged and tugged the old machine halfway up the cellar stairs, where Hugo, investigating, discovered them; he completed the portage by himself as easily as if it had been Hiawatha's canoe.

Hugo deposited the Victrola in the parlor and tracked down a pot of usable grease; he came back with the pot and the records, and Keith set about cleaning and regreasing the machine, while Lynn went through the box, sorting the records and dusting them. There was even a packet of steel needles in the box, miraculously never opened. Keith began to crank.

" 'On the Tamiami Trail,' " Lynn read one label. "I never heard of it."

"I have," Richard Queen said. And, as the Victrola burst into scratchy, faraway song, he said formally, "Mrs. Queen, may I have the pleasure?"

Before Jessie could jump to her feet the music stopped with a dying screech, and Richard turned in protest to find Vaughn straightening up from the machine, leering over his rape like a Vandal, while old Hendrik stood in the doorway, smiling. He had a thin portfolio tucked under one arm.

"You'll have to postpone your dance for some other occasion, Inspector. This time I'm calling the meeting."

He felt his way to his favorite chair and settled himself. Hugo moved a low table to a position before the chair. The old man patted the table, nodded, and placed the portfolio on it. Vaughn and Hugo took up a rather ominous stand flanking the chair.

"It's two weeks or thereabouts since the attempt on my life was made by—as Inspector Queen would put it—person or persons unknown," the old man began in his lip-smacking way, "but here I am still alive and kicking, as they say, and here you all still are, waiting on the old lunatic's decision. Well, I've decided."

DeWitt Alistair inclined his head as if listening for distant drums. Elizabeth Alistair sat steady as an Indian chief, but the Inspector noticed that she was holding her breath. So she belonged to the human race after all.

"I don't hear anything," the old man said. "You're wondering now what the old fool's going to say. How many of us? Eh? Which of us? Who gets? And who doesn't? Well, ladies and gentlemen, my conclusion is that there's not much to choose among you."

And this smells high to heaven, Richard Queen told him in the voiceless colloquy he was conducting. Alistair was an all-round no-goodnik, and Mrs. Alistair was about as attractive as Sinjanthropus's wife. And to claim that there was little to choose as between, say, Lynn O'Neill and Cornelia Openshaw was the clearest example of blindness he had yet seen in the blind man.

Brass rapped on the floor. "I've instructed Mr. Vaughn, in his capacity as Attorney Vaughn, to draw up my will, and he has done so."

"Yes?" burst out Miss Openshaw, and put her purple-tipped claws to her mouth.

"Ah, my dear, can't wait? I understand. You see how much good your meddling's done, Inspector? Why, ladies and gentlemen, I have left my estate—all six million dollars' worth, as advertised—to the six of you, share and share alike. How's that?"

There were sighs, signifying thankfulness. The Inspector felt let down. He had had some wild thought that the old man meant to set his prisoners to springing at one another's throats by leaving some of them out; but who, with the possible exception of DeWitt Alistair, would resent sharing a gratuitous fortune with five other people when each share was worth $1,000,000?

"However," said the old man, and paused.

Ah, the Inspector thought.

"There's a proviso. I told you that Mr. Vaughn was not able to locate another of my candidates, the person named Harding Boyle. Well, if Boyle should turn up no later than one month after my death, he will be included as an equal legatee, so that the estate would then be split seven ways instead of six. Oh, yes, and I have left a special bequest in my will to Mr. Zarbus."

"To *who*?" asked the Inspector, his grammar showing.

"Zarbus, Hugo Zarbus, O good and faithful servant, et cetera. This dumbhead here. It won't much affect anyone's share, however; you can afford to be generous."

Why can't I believe a word the old rascal says? the Inspector demanded of himself in despair. Maybe it was the result of a total misreading of superficial signs—of the mendacious way old Brass chomped, sucked, leered; the derisive chuckle and titter. Could it be that this appearance of insincerity had nothing to do with his character? After all, he was rewarding the man who had cooked his meals, polished his tons of brass, taken care of his creature needs, suffered his abuse, day in and out for years. The Inspector shook his head. He simply could not see Hendrik Brass being grateful to anyone for anything. No, there was a gimmick in all this. Only what was it?

As for Hugo Zarbus, the announcement of his windfall left him looking exactly as stupid as he always looked.

The old man was opening the portfolio. From it he took a blue-backed document and spread it flat.

"Mr. Vaughn, will you ask Sarah and Emma Hotaling to step in here?"

Vaughn said nothing nastily and went away. He returned herding the two women Brass had hired for the duration of his visitors' stay. The Hotaling sisters were Phillipskill spinsters who seemed to have been born frightened. They crept about the premises making beds and pretending to dust, and all but ran after the dinner dishes were put away; they never left without giving the impression that they were not coming back. But they did. So Brass must be paying them. But where was he getting the money? He must have some hidden away, probably in the same cache from which he had taken the $100 and $1000 bills.

"A pen, Mr. Vaughn."

Vaughn produced a ballpoint pen and placed it in the old man's hand.

"Guide me to the signature line."

The private detective-lawyer set the hand in place.

"Sarah and Emma," Hendrik Brass said, "I am now going to sign my will. I ask you to witness. Do you understand what I'm talking about?"

The two women nodded in terror.

He wrote laboriously. There was no sound but the swish of the pen.

"Now, Mr. Vaughn, have the Misses Hotaling sign as witnesses."

The sisters frantically wrote their names where Vaughn's stabbing finger indicated.

"By God," Vaughn drawled, "they can write."

"Are they finished, Mr. Vaughn?"

"Yup."

"Then thank you, ladies. That's all."

Under cover of the sisters' flight, the Inspector drifted across the room to glance down at the will. Vaughn was watching him with a grin. But there was no question that the "Hendrik Brass" the old man had shakily written was in the same hand as the signature in Jessie's letter of invitation.

"That's enough, dad," Vaughn said, and picked up the will. "You'll wear the ink out. Anything else, Mr. Brass?"

"One thing. You people need be in no hurry to leave. In fact, I should like you all to stay on. Eat! Drink! Be merry! For who knows? Tomorrow the old man may die, and then you'd only have to come back. But with what a difference, eh? Rich! Does my heart good to think of it. Ah, what a wonderful thing it is to give. The question is, will I receive?"

The cackle this time was prolonged. He sounded exactly like Basil Rathbone's Witch in the "Hansel and Gretel" recording the Inspector had once given Wes Polonsky's daughter's firstborn.

"Of course, if you want to go . . ."

It seemed to the Inspector that Brass allowed his voice to dribble out deliberately. *If you want to go . . .* Then what happens?

"Look, Mr. Brass," the Inspector said. "Wouldn't this be a good time to let these folks know just where your money is? If you've got it tucked away somewhere, it might put everybody to a lot of trouble trying to find it. Not to anticipate your death, but you brought the subject up yourself."

He could have sworn that the sunken eyes in their liverish pits saw him.

"Giving you a bad time, Inspector? Well, sir, I don't choose to tell you. No sir. What do you think of that?"

He chuckled and held out his arm to Hugo.

They heard the old man complaining all the way upstairs, Vaughn stalking behind; whining that Hugo was going too fast, too slowly, too clumsily, until the querulous voice was cut off by the snip of a door.

"Well?" Richard demanded. "You people going or staying?"

Young Palmer was rubbing his hands. "He seems to want us to stay. Far as I'm concerned old Hendrik can do no wrong—not after today! How about you, Lynn?"

"I've nowhere to go, and I'm in no hurry to get there." Lynn wriggled. "Golly! A whole million dollars!"

"I wonder," wondered Cornelia with Chinese eyes, "where he's hiding it."

"That's his hook," the Inspector said wearily. "He's playing you people like fish. He's got some cockeyed reason for wanting you here. In my book that's good enough reason to get out."

"Then you're leaving?" Dr. Thornton asked.

"Somebody has to watch over you babes in the woods. Who knows what's in that head of his?"

"I noticed he didn't say anything this time about giving us the other half of the $1000 bill if we left," the doctor muttered. "Well, I've invested this much time, I'll stick a few days longer."

"You, Alistair?"

The beefy man did not hesitate. "If I had dough, I'd say this was some crazy con. But Liz and I are kind of on the short side. I'm playing the hand out."

To which Mrs. Alistair nodded.

"In that case," Richard said to his tender half, who had been sitting there having the creeping shivers over the mess she had got them into, "we may as well take up where we left off. Miss O'Neill, would you put the phonograph back on?"

And to the scratchy strains of "On the Tamiami Trail" he grabbed Jessie around the waist, swept her out into the middle of the parlor, and launched into a Warren G. Harding-type foxtrot.

"We'd better be getting back, Mr. Palmer," Lynn said. "That moon is doing things to you."

Keith mumbled something. He turned off the portable radio he had bought in Tarrytown and scrambled to his feet. The moon was sending a message across the Hudson that ended gloriously at the half-sunken dock. But then it had touched Lynn, too. Maybe she was immune.

Lynn took his arm cosily as they strolled back.

He wished she wouldn't. It brought them into contact. Of course, contact was what he wanted more than anything, but what good was contact without cooperation?

So he walked stiffly. Lynn did not seem to notice. She kept chattering away about an insurance guy named Harry, the wonders of food processing, and other memorabilia of Wagon Springs. That last kiss had been something all right. But from the way Lynn was acting, it might never have happened. Maybe the music had been wrong. The jockey had put on Zero Mostel. Keith cursed himself. He had tried to find some schmaltzy love songs on the transistor, but no dice.

"What?" Keith said. She had broken contact. He felt a sense of inconsolable loss.

"I left my purse down at the dock, darn it. We'll have to go back."

"Oh. I'll go. You wait." He plunged off, taking the flashlight with him. Why, the poor guy, Lynn thought. Leaving me without a light in the woods. I did get him flustered.

She rapped her shin against a big rock and sat down, rubbing her leg.

In the dark.

In the very dark.

It was so dark suddenly that Lynn began to be furious. Getting him hot and bothered was lovely, but this smacked of petty male revenge, which wasn't in the rule book. I'll make him pay, Lynn thought, and immediately felt better.

Light blinded her.

"Hi, babe," said the voice behind it.

Vaughn's voice.

Lynn leaped. But he was too quick for her. She felt herself smothered, surrounded, immobilized, befouled. His hands were everywhere. She squirmed and tried to kick and bite. He laughed. He was not even breathing hard.

"Yup," Vaughn said. "You feel even better than I thought you would."

Lynn tried to scream. But he had his forearm against her throat.

"Now you don't mean that, baby," Vaughn said. He began gently to bend her backward. "Yell your head off. I like it that way."

"Wait, wait!"

"Why fight it, baby? If you can put out for a square like Palmer, think what a real man'll feel like."

He must be vulnerable somewhere, Lynn thought desperately. "I thought . . . you had . . . a job guarding Mr. Brass."

"Beddy-bye behind a locked door. Quit stalling, chick, and awayyyyyyy we go."

The next thing Lynn knew she was flat on her back and he was straddling her. He looked twenty feet tall. Lynn gathered all the breath in her body and shrieked, *"Keith!"*

Keith was coming on the run. She could hear his big feet crashing through the brush. A crazy light began bobbing in her direction. Lynn rolled over and away. Vaughn swore, and laughed, and turned off his flash. Lynn shut her eyes. Poor Keith. Now, on top of everything else, he was going to take a beating. For her. Vaughn would break him in two. How he would hate her. Oh, Lynn. She found herself crouching behind a tree, afraid to look.

She heard sounds. Feet sounds, nose sounds, lung sounds, fist sounds, and finally whole body sounds. Then no sounds.

I'd better start running, Lynn thought dully.

But then a man came around the tree and took her arm roughly and said, "Tough boy won't bother you anymore. I found out something."

Thank you, God.

"Oh, Keith, he gave you a bloody nose!"

"Hell, no. I ran into a tree coming up the path."

"Found out?" Lynn found herself hugging him. "Found out what?"

But Keith seemed remote in a manly, majestic sort of way. "The guy has a glass jaw."

As soon as Richard locked and bolted their door that night, Jessie said, "Richard, I want to get out of this. I mean it."

"Palmer took him," her husband said, shaking his head. "I'll be damned."

"First thing tomorrow morning I'm going to that old man and tell him his monster Vaughn made a mistake in my case. Then, darling, we're *leaving*."

"What? Oh, no, not yet, hon." He was frowning. "We can't. At least I can't. But I wish you would."

"Richard Queen, I'm your excuse for being here. You know I won't go one foot without you."

"You're a stubborn woman."

"You're a—you're a policeman!"

"Honey, I think we're in for a rough time. That will Brass had Vaughn draw up was a bad mistake. He's practically asking for it."

"Asking for what?"

"A box and six feet of Westchester County. You mark my words, Jessie. With this setup, the will that old idiot signed today is going to be his death warrant."

Two days later he was proved a prophet.

6

WHO?

The evening before had been remarkable in only one respect. The Queens encountered Hugo on their before-dinner walk back from the woods. He was an extraordinary sight. He was dressed in a blue serge suit that fitted him like a coat of mail and trailed whiffs of mothballs; enormous oxblood-colored shoes; and what in the Inspector's youth had been called an "iron hat"—a derby. And he was chugging out of the driveway on an aged Honda.

Hugo braked, and the Inspector asked gravely, "Where you going all dressed up? Got a date?" He tried to visualize the female who would date Hugo, and could not.

"It is my night off, Mr. Queen," Hugo said proudly. "Mr. Hendrik gives me four whole nights off a year."

"Can he spare 'em?"

"Have a nice time," Jessie said; and Hugo tipped his derby and chugged on his way. "Poor man. Why, Richard, it's practically *slavery*."

"He must get paid something if he can afford to go to town. Wonder where he goes. And what he does."

"And how little," Jessie said grimly, "Mr. Brass pays him."

Mr. Brass seemed out of sorts at the dinner table. The Inspector put it down to Hugo's absence. The old man was neither japish nor tittery tonight; for the most part he munched in silence, feeling around for his food. Occasionally Vaughn, who was still showing a purpled souvenir on the southeast corner of his jaw, speared a slippery piece of meat for him. Once Brass called testily for wine, and Vaughn went down to the cellar and came up with a tall dark slender bottle, stagily dusty and cobwebbed. The old man fingered it and sniffed at the cork.

"This claret is older than I am," he squeaked. "Always meant to keep it for an occasion. Ah, well, who knows? Fill my glass, Mr. Vaughn. And the others'."

They sipped to Hendrik Brass's health. He seemed to derive a derisive pleasure out of that, and cocked his head evilly at them in turn, looking more like himself. The claret had turned to vinegar, and none of them finished it. Shortly afterward Vaughn took the old man up to bed. In the flicker of the candles the wine left in their glasses sparkled like fresh blood.

The Inspector found himself sitting up in bed, every nerve alert. Beside him Jessie slept. He listened, wondering why. No wind rattled branches outdoors or made the old house groan; no one had cried out—he was sure of that. Yet he had been awakened by something.

He slipped into his robe and slippers and noiselessly unlocked and unlatched the bedroom door and stepped out into the chill hall. The red night light was a misty wound in the shadows. He strained his eyes in the grayness, and his ears. He could just make out the big blob down the hall before Hendrik Brass's door that was Vaughn, lying on his guardian cot.

Then he heard it clearly. It was Vaughn snoring. Of course. The man had to sleep, and the Inspector had made no sound. Still, he thought, I could tiptoe up to him and put him out of commission before he could reach for his gun. Maybe Keith's haymaker to his jaw had taken the starch out of him; he certainly had been acting sheepish since the battle in the woods.

Suddenly the short hairs on the Inspector's neck rose and a cold finger ran down his spine. Those were no snores he heard, but the rough and broken sounds of a struggle for breath.

He began to run.

Once more Dr. Thornton and Jessie Sherwood Queen tended a patient, sponged blood, administered hypos, and sutured and dressed a wound.

"He's lucky," Thornton said. "In spite of all his boozing he's in good shape. He'll be all right."

Lynn O'Neill, who had been staring fascinated at her sedated attacker of two days before, said, "And Mr. Brass?" She moistened her young lips.

"Mr. Brass," Dr. Thornton muttered, "is dead."

Keith Palmer said, "Lynn, I'd better get you out of here."

He took her away. The others were in the hall, where Chief Fleck had sent them.

Fleck licked his lips, too. There was triumph in his small eyes, and anticipation, and the hope of many, many reporters. He asked jovially, "Could this Vaughn have stabbed himself?"

Thornton shook his head.

"Impossible," the Inspector said. "The angle of the wound shows that he was stabbed from behind as he lay on his side facing the door. The knife slid in under his shoulder blade at an upward angle. He couldn't have done it himself if he were a contortionist."

Jessie fastened the last strip of adhesive tape across the man's naked, hairy back. They had put him on the couch in old Brass's sitting room. In the adjoining bedroom the last of the Brasses lay dead in his tall brass bed. There was no doubt that he had died in it. There was also no doubt that he had been murdered in it.

The Phillipskill police chief stalked back into the bedroom for another look. Richard and Dr. Thornton followed, leaving Jessie with the sedated Vaughn.

Hendrik Brass's eyes glared up at his wrinkled ceiling, as blind in death as they had been in life. The mouth gaped toothless—his dentures were in a glass beside the bed—gray-blue as the gray-blue face. It seemed to the Inspector that he was smiling, enjoying his joke to the end, and beyond. The blade that pinned his bloody nightshirt to his flesh was buried to the haft.

"County Medical Examiner's M.D. ought to been here long ago," Chief Fleck grumbled. "What's your opinion, Dr. Thornton?"

"I could tell more if I removed the knife."

"Then do it. I authorize you. But be careful about prints."

Thornton was still wearing surgical gloves. He grasped the ends of the crosspiece, avoiding the haft, and lifted gently. The knife came out of Hendrik Brass's heart as if it had impaled a piece of cheese. A trickle of blood oozed out, and stopped.

"Brass," Richard said. "What else?"

It was all of brass, and it was rather short—although it had been long enough—and the blade as well as the handle was intricately chased with the tiny crucibles and other symbols with which its owner had seemed obsessed. Thornton scrutinized the blade, its length, its shape.

"My guess is it's the same blade that wounded Vaughn. And of course it's what killed Brass, though the autopsy will make sure of that. Unless there's one just like it around somewhere."

"I saw this one—or its double—on Brass's desk downstairs as late as last night," the Inspector said.

Fleck's man, who had been dusting the room for prints, was sent below. He came back shaking his head. "It's not there now, Vic."

"Then this is the one, all right. I wonder what kind of knife it is. Never saw one like it." Fleck's little eyes sought Richard Queen's, and looked away.

"It's a fancy letter opener," Richard said. "And it was on his desk in plain sight. Anyone could have taken it."

"Then it's probably another inside job, like that hit over the head a couple weeks back." The police chief glanced about. "Oh, Doc," he said, relieved. "Looks like I've drawn a big one at last."

And the Inspector knew that Chief Victor Fleck had no intention of turning the case over to a higher authority. He had probably not even notified the State Police; no troopers had shown up. He wondered if Fleck would even call on their crime laboratory facilities. He would fight tooth and nail to keep on top of the case; he must have visions of himself running for Sheriff out of the publicity.

Richard turned to the newcomer.

The Medical Examiner's physician was a brisk, balding young man with tired eyes who seemed to know Chief Fleck of old. He nodded curtly, said nothing, and set about his examination. He paid no attention to the others.

The chief's man looked up from the letter knife. "No prints I can raise, Vic. Either they won't take on all this engraving, or whoever used it wore gloves."

"Tag it for the files, Bob, after Dr. Ash gets through with it. I guess we've pulled a cute one. Well, Doc?"

The country doctor straightened up. "Is that the knife?"

"It's the one we took out of his chest."

Dr. Ash looked it over. "I'll take it along for comparison purposes during the P.M., but it certainly looks as if it did the job. I'll arrange for removal of the body."

"Do you have to take him to the county seat?"

"Where do you suggest I do the autopsy, Chief, on this bed? Sure I have to."

"Well, all right."

"Dr. Ash," said the Inspector.

"Yes?"

"How long would you say he's been dead?"

"Yeah," said Fleck, fast. "How long, Doc?"

"I may know more exactly after the post, but my preliminary opinion is that he died between four and six this morning." He jerked the topsheet over the dead man's head and brusquely left.

"How's it sound to you, Thornton?" the chief demanded.

"Between four and six A.M., yes."

"Then it looks pretty clear to me. Middle of the night, and Vaughn was sleeping on the cot across the old man's doorway. Whoever committed this crime sneaked up on Vaughn in the dark, stuck the knife in his back, pulled it out, and got into Brass's bedroom and let the old man have it with the same knife. That stack up to you, Queen?"

"Sounds likely."

They found the private detective sitting up on the couch, and Jessie breathing indignation.

"He won't do a thing I tell him to, Doctor," she said. "He actually wants to get up!"

Vaughn took the flask from his lips and cursed. "She tells me the old man got it in the heart. Who the hell got past me?"

"That's what you'd better answer, mister," Fleck said.

Vaughn gave him the fish eye. "Who are you? The local fuzz, I suppose. How do I know who it was? I was catching some shuteye." His arms flexed, and he winced. "When I catch the joker who stuck that shiv in me—"

"Any notion who might have done it?"

"Fanny Farmer. How do I know? I was sleeping, I tell you—"

"Sleeping off a drunk, if you ask me," the Inspector said. "How many belts did you have last night?"

Vaughn chose to ignore him. "Look, fuzz," he said to Fleck. "Old man Brass was my job. You haul your fallen arches back to Phillipskill and give some Joe Tourist a speeding ticket. Leave this caper to me. When I've got him I'll dump him in your lap. If he'll fit under your front porch, that is."

Fleck's face had turned from red to purple.

"You want to see the inside of my pokey? Watch that big mouth when you talk to me!"

"Look," Vaughn sneered, "I happen to be a lawyer, and I specialize in suits for false arrest. So cool it, man. Damn it, Thornton, this dressing stinks. I can feel myself bleeding again."

"If you'd remained quiet, as Mrs. Queen told you to," Thornton snapped, "it wouldn't be. We'll have to redress it. It's all right, Chief, I can handle him. If he gets tough, I'll just yank on a suture."

They left Vaughn with Thornton and Jessie, Fleck raging. He bellowed for his other assistant, a crosseyed man he called Lew, and ordered him to watch Vaughn. "If he gives you any trouble, slap him in cuffs!"

"What are you going to do now, Chief?" the Inspector asked. He was genuinely curious.

"Find out where everybody was," the chief said, glaring. "Starting with you."

It was a wary group that Fleck assembled downstairs.

Everyone but Palmer was in a robe. Everyone was watchful. Everyone spoke with loving care. Over the parlor and its lively brass hovered the spirit of $6,000,000. Someone there had hastened the great day, and he—or she, or they—meant to survive undetected to enjoy its reward. The Inspector, sensitive to such atmospheres, felt it in every cell. Poor Jessie could only sit and shiver in the chill of morning.

"Between four and six?" Ellery's father said. "That's a bad time to have to prove an alibi. I was in bed with my wife. It had already happened when I got up to see what had wakened me. Mrs. Queen was sleeping."

"Not when you got out of bed," Jessie said. "After all those years as a nurse I sleep with one eye open. I saw my husband get up and go out, Chief."

"What time was that?" Fleck wanted to know. And added hopefully, "I suppose you didn't notice?"

"Yes, I did. I always wear my watch to bed, and as you can see it has a radium dial. Part of my training, too. It was seven minutes past six."

Fleck grunted. "How about you, Miss O'Neill?"

Lynn looked angry. "I wish I could prove I was sleeping. But I was, even if I can't. Sleeping like mad. I always do. I didn't even know anything was wrong till all the noise this morning woke me up."

"You, Palmer?"

"Sleeping," Keith said. "The noise woke me, too. Inspector Queen asked me to get to a phone and notify you, so I dressed and did. That's all I know."

"Miss Openshaw? Can you prove where you were between four and six A.M.?"

"What do you think I am?" Cornelia asked in shrill outrage. "I was alone in my bed. Where else would I be? I'm a decent woman, I'll have you know!"

"No alibi, either. You, Mr. Alistair?" He looks like a Met fan after the last out, the Inspector thought. Fleck had come to the game expecting a home run first man up.

Just a shade too quickly Alistair said, "My wife and I were like the Queens, Chief, in bed together."

"That," said Hube Thornton, "is a damn lie."

From Mrs. Alistair's look at Thornton, Richard expected him to slide to the floor at their feet. But the doctor merely said to Fleck, "I'm a restless sleeper, and I woke up about three o'clock. So I read a medical journal I'd been meaning to get caught up on. At half-past three or so I heard noise from the Alistairs' room, which is next to mine. A few minutes later I heard their door open and close. I wondered what was going on and got out of bed and opened my door. I saw Alistair pussyfooting it down the hall. He disappeared around the corner and I went back to bed."

Chief Fleck said, "Aha!" The Inspector could not believe his ears. "Why didn't you yell?"

"For what? I hadn't seen him do anything, and I knew Vaughn was stretched out across the door to Brass's room. He's been doing it every night. But I definitely saw Alistair leave his room."

"So you lied," Fleck shouted at Alistair. "That's going to cost you, mister!"

The country squire was not florid now. But his voice was persuasive. "I didn't want to get involved, Chief. You can understand that, after what's happened. It was a mistake, I see that now. I'm sorry."

"Where did you go?"

"I've suffered from insomnia all my life. Last night it was particularly bad. So I got up and put on my robe and slippers and slipped out of the house for some air. This damn place is like a tomb."

"What did you do out there?"

"Just walked. In the woods. At one point I went down to the boat landing. Sat smoking there till dawn. I got back a few minutes to six and fell right asleep. I didn't wake up till my wife shook me and told me the news."

Smooth as snake oil, Elizabeth Alistair said, "I heard my husband get up, and I heard him come back. I'm a light sleeper, too. It's just as DeWitt says."

"Except you can't prove he spent all that time at the landing," Fleck said. "Or where you were, Mrs. Alistair!"

"In *bed*."

"Alone. Between four and six. Nobody has an alibi, not even you, Queen—you know yourself the police don't give house room to a husband and wife alibiing each other. The only one caught lying outright is Alistair, and I'm tucking that away, mister, in my little black book." Alistair looked displeased; his wife looked deadly. "Oh, Hugo. How are you? Feeling any better?"

Fleck could only have said it out of some crude fellow-countryman kindness. Hugo looked as if he had had a memorable night. His derby was missing, but he was still in his blue serge suit and oxblood shoes. The suit was rumpled and dirty and gave off a strong malty odor; the shoes were scuffed; one lace trailed. The little eyes were red-veined and puffed, the huge jaw shaking.

He was suffering from hangover as well as grief; they had found him sprawled on his bed, fully dressed, snoring like a whale and smelling like a brewery after his night in town.

Fleck had questioned him, but he remembered nothing. He had gone to a tavern outside Phillipskill and performed prodigies of beer consumption. He did not recall leaving the tavern, or getting home, or where his Honda was (they found it near the entrance to the Brass property, where he had evidently fallen off). And as far as time was concerned, it had not existed for him.

Hugo did not answer Chief Fleck's question at once. He rubbed his bushy massif of a jaw as if he had a toothache, and he said in his *basso vibrato*, "Mr. Hendrik is dead. Oh, he is dead." Then he answered it. "And my head hurts."

"I'm leaving my two men here till I finish my investigation," Fleck announced before he drove off, "and nobody better try to cop out, because I'll take it hard. Don't leave the grounds, except if you need anything from town one of the ladies can do it. Oh, and if anybody decides he's got something to say to me, tell one of my officers. Okay?" Then he left, almost skipping.

There was nothing else. No fingerprints had been found in Brass's sitting room or bedroom—or on the door Vaughn had been straddling—that should not have been there. No evidence of any description had turned up. They were immured with a murderer, and the Inspector felt challenged.

"But Richard dear," Jessie protested, "all we have to do is tell Chief Fleck I'm not the real Jessie Sherwood and he'll let us go. He'll know *we* can't be mixed up with that six million dollars. I see no reason to stay on. We're not even able to help that poor old man anymore."

That was when her spouse took her hands in his and said, "Honey, I've got to hear the other shoe drop. One of these people murdered old Hendrik. Who? I can't leave till I find out."

So all Jessie could do was stand at her bedroom window and watch the county meat wagon cart away the remains of their baffling host, dissection-table-bound. There were other faces at other windows, all glum, watching, too. Even if the late Hendrik had died fortified by the prayers of the Dutch Reformed Church (which he had told them in his wicked way he had not attended for sixty years), they would not have felt comforted. Not, at least, until the pall of murder was lifted from The House of Brass; or for relief, the six million untraced dollars were dealt among the lucky innocents.

And that seemed a long way off, for Vaughn in his legal entity assured them that the law debarred any distribution of the estate for at least six months. He seemed to take joy in the assurance.

It occurred to more than one of them that, suddenly, in some magical reversal of reality, they had exchanged one tormentor for another.

7

AND WHERE AGAIN?

Burial was to be in the family plot on the grounds at Hendrik Brass's express request, Vaughn said. "He told me F.D.R. got planted in his Hyde Park turf, and he had as much right to dig his own dirt as any Democrat that ever died."

"May I inquire," inquired Mr. Pealing of Pealing & Pealing, the Phillipskill morticians, "if the deceased left any provision—?"

"If you mean you're buggered about your bread, Mac," Vaughn said, "I wouldn't advise making with the super-deluxe bronze. There's some question about the scratch. The best I can promise you right now is that your bill will give you a creditor's claim on the estate."

"No insurance policies, Mr. Vaughn?"

"No policies."

Mr. Pealing sighed. "Well, my father buried his father, and my grandfather buried his grandfather, so I suppose I can't do less than bury him. And if the estate can't settle the bill, we'll write it off to goodwill." Mr. Pealing allowed himself to smile at this.

"I never met a body snatcher yet who'd give you the scraps out of his embalming pail. You'll deduct it from your income tax."

Mr. Pealing retreated.

"Why do you have to be so unpleasant to everybody, Mr. Vaughn?" asked Jessie. "Mr. Pealing said that out of the goodness of his heart."

"That noblesse oblige crud?" Vaughn laughed and went about his business, which at the moment was to make Hugo's life even more miserable than it was.

The old Sleepy Hollow Church had been shut down for years except for an annual service, to Jessie's disappointment;

but the police chief vetoed any church rites, and the funeral was held from the house. The modest casket was not opened. The only outsiders present were a Tarrytown minister, Mr. Pealing and an assistant, and Chief Fleck's crosseyed Lew. The small Brass graveyard in its hollow near the road was a thicket of triumphant weeds and leaning stones, some with gasping cherubim on them; a sumac had planted itself before the doorway of the single half-ruined mausoleum. The minister read a simple service, watched Hugo and the undertaker's assistant fill in the grave, shook hands, and fled. The others followed suit, all but Richard and Jessie, who lingered among the stones, stepping over those that had fallen, reading all but obliterated epitaphs, and after a while clasping hands for communication.

The stone that sent them hurrying back to the house was a thin slab, sandy brown, on which were incised the words POMPEY—*Faithful Unto Death.* As Jessie remarked, Pompey might as well have been a horse.

They found Fleck waiting in the parlor with the others. The Inspector grinned. The chief had been playing it with coziness. Not a newsman had shown up; there had been no mention in the local papers of old Brass's murder, only of his death. Fleck was sitting on the homicide, saving the news for the great day when he could announce not only that it had taken place, but that he had solved it.

The chief sat very still before the fireplace, as if in hope that its dimensions would diminish him. He took no part in what followed.

Vaughn said, "Settle down, boys and girls. *Vino* on the house. We've guzzled the last of that lousy claret, today we polish off the port, and what's left downstairs wouldn't make a vinegar dressing. Anybody want to hear decedent's last legal words?"

He had slipped a soiled T-shirt over his bandages; only a slight brown tear under his right shoulder blade and a certain caution of gesture reminded of his stab wound. His shoulder holster with its nuzzling .38 was very much in evidence. He opened the blue-backed will.

It began, "I, Hendrik Simon Brass, a single man, of the Town of Phillipskill, County of Westchester, State of New York, being in full possession of my faculties, but sensible of the uncertainties of this mortal life . . ."

So he dictated the wording, the Inspector decided. It was the Brass style, all right. He noticed that no one was reaching for the port.

Vaughn read through the appetizers. After a while he got

to the meat, and paused for their slavering benefit. Then he laughed and read on.

"I give and devise to my manservant, Hugo Zarbus, my house and lands situate in the Town of Phillipskill.

"The remainder and residue of my estate I give and bequeath to DeWitt Alistair, Lynn O'Neill, Cornelia Openshaw, Keith Palmer, Jessie Sherwood, and Hubert Thornton, share and share alike, if living at my decease.

"If by the expiration of one month after my death one Harding Boyle, whereabouts unknown to me, shall appear in his person and make claim to participation in my estate, he shall receive an equal share with the six legatees named in the paragraph preceding. The executor of my estate shall have full authority to identify the said Harding Boyle and to certify his claim or reject it.

"At the expiration of the one month above-mentioned, the contents of my house and outbuildings shall be sold at public auction for the benefit of the residuary heirs.

"I nominate herewith, and appoint as executor of my estate free of bond, my attorney Vaughn J. Vaughn . . ."

When Vaughn J. Vaughn had concluded, there was a fascinated hush. Then Richard Queen said, "That's one daisy of a will, Vaughn. What kind of lawyer are you? Nothing is said about payment of debts. Nothing is said about the value of the residuary estate or, more important, what it consists of—"

"Or where it is!" screeched Cornelia Openshaw. "You drew up this will. Where is it?"

Vaughn poured himself a slug of port, shrugged, winced, and tossed the wine down. "Don't ask me, baby."

"And don't you 'baby' me! I want to know what I've just inherited. I have a *right* to know. He named you his executor. You've *got* to know!"

"All I know is what I just read in the paper."

Alistair was trembling. He said in a very flat voice, "Look, Vaughn, you know what's at stake here—"

"You certainly do," Lynn said. "Do you mean to tell us that Mr. Brass didn't tell you where his fortune is?"

"Brass was an old mule. He insisted on dictating the will word for word. When I suggested ordinary legal additions he wouldn't listen. When I asked him to specify what his estate consists of and where the six million dollars' worth is, he cackled and clammed up. Anything else you want to know, friends, consult a crystal ball. Tennis, anyone?"

At that moment Lew came in and whispered to his chief. Fleck got up heavily and went out and a moment later came back with two men. One was fat, the other was thin. Both had eyes like pack rats.

"Mr. Fluegle and Mr. Channing," Fleck said. "Lawyers from Phillipskill. You can take it from there." And he squeezed himself before the fireplace again.

Mr. Fluegle said in a fat voice, "I represent the creditors of the late Hendrik Brass in Phillipskill."

Mr. Channing said in a thin voice. "*I* represent the creditors of the late Hendrik Brass in Phillipskill."

Mr. Fluegle glared at Mr. Channing. "You didn't lose any time getting here."

Mr. Channing spat at Mr. Fluegle, "And ditto!"

"Now, girls," Vaughn said. "I'm the late etcetera's executor and I dig you've split the wolf pack between you. Where are the tabs and how much do they come to?"

Each lawyer produced a briefcaseful of bills. They thrust them at Vaughn in a dead heat.

Vaughn riffled through them. "Gas, electric, hardware, butcher, baker—I suppose there'd be a candlestick-maker if Brass hadn't made his own. And so on far into the night. How much does your clients' share of the loot come to, Fatty?"

Mr. Fluegle said, "$3,025.11."

"Skinny?"

Mr. Channing snapped, "$4,443.13."

Vaughn pushed the wine aside, produced his flask, unscrewed the cap, and threw his head back. When it had sought its level again he said, "This here lightning calculator makes that $7,468.24, right, pardners? Well, all valid claims will be settled in full when that fathead police chief over there lets me out of here long enough to file the will. Assuming, of course, there are assets sufficient to cover them, on which point said executor has no scuttle yet. Any other remarks? Don't bother. Hugo, heave these bloodsuckers out."

Hugo blinked. Then he advanced on the two lawyers, rather like a glacier. They departed with all deliberate speed.

Vaughn took another pull on the inexhaustible flask. (He must have brought a case with him, the Inspector thought.) "Come on, cats, you're sitting around here looking like you're in the same bag. Get with it. Who's going to start the action?"

"I'll do it," Richard said. "For openers, I point out that the will makes no provision for maintenance of the house or us during the month waiting period. The stores certainly aren't going to extend any more credit, nor after what those lawyers just heard. If we stay on here we've got to have power and we've got to have food. Looks to me as if we're going to have to pool our resources."

"*If* we stay on, Cornelia said bitterly, "and *if* Hugo doesn't mind. It's his house now."

"At least he knows what *he* inherited," Keith said.

"What Hugo inherited," the Inspector said, "is the doubtful equity in a twice-mortgaged piece of property nobody would take as a gift. Do you mind, Hugo?"

Hugo looked frightened. "Mind, Mr. Queen?" he said nervously. "Mind what?"

"Don't waste your time talking to dickybird," Vaughn said. "Anyway, nothing is anybody's till the will goes through probate and all claims on the estate are settled, which is going to take at least six months, as I told you, more likely a year. If you squares want to toss your bread around supporting this pad, it's okay by me, but my advice is to go home and wait for what the Surrogate and Allah provide."

"That would be good advice," the Inspector said, "except for two little details."

"What's one, dad?"

"Brass was murdered. Fleck won't let us go."

Chief Fleck stirred and nodded cautiously.

"And the other one?"

"I can't believe that Brass didn't say *something* about the whereabouts of that alleged six million."

"I agree," Dr. Thornton said. "He was having too much fun mystifying us not to have left some clue, even if it was cryptic."

"You holding out on us, Vaughn?" Alistair said, his voice even flatter than before.

Rather slyly, the Inspector thought without charity, Vaughn began to act as if he were in pain. "Sheest!" he said, grimacing. "This air hole in my back hurts like hell. You sure you didn't get your degree in dentistry, Doc?"

"You're lucky to be walking around," Thornton growled. "And don't try to change the subject. Just what did the old man say?"

"Nothing, I tell you. Nothing that means anything."

It was Elizabeth Alistair who got the first exclamation in. "Then he did tell you something! What?"

Vaughn shrugged and winced again. "He said it was somewhere in the building."

"This building?" Lynn cried.

"This building."

"But where?" Cornelia Openshaw demanded.

"I asked him. He wouldn't say." He got to his feet. "Doc,

my back's crucifying me. How about some pain killer? I don't even smoke grass."

"Damn Hippocrates," Dr. Thornton muttered. "Hugo, help me get this hood upstairs."

When Thornton returned, the Inspector said, "We've been waiting for you, Doctor. We've agreed some kind of action has to be taken. Chief Fleck has the right to say yes or no to whatever we decide on, of course. He's said he'd at least listen. That right, Chief?"

Fleck's barnyard eyes were muddy with suspicion. He said, "Yes?" Then he said, "Yes." Then he said, "Depends on what action."

"I know what I'd do," Cornelia said viciously. "You men ought to take that *thing* upstairs down to the cellar and thrash him. He knows more than he's letting on. Beat it out of him!"

"What action?" Fleck repeated.

"One step ought to be taken right away," Richard said. "According to Vaughn, Brass said the six million—in whatever form it is—is somewhere in this house. We have to search the house." He held up his hand at their cries of enthusiasm. "It's no job for amateurs. Not if it's to be done right. Chief, I have five old cronies, retired from the force like me, who've been helping me out in this merry-go-round. With your permission I'd like to make up a search party of myself, you, your own officers, and my five friends. They're pros, and they won't want a thing out of it but to get off their duffs. What do you say?"

The chief looked at him, pondering ponderously.

"And if there's any trouble with Vaughn about it," the Inspector added in a helpless way that made Jessie want to pinch his perfidious hide, "why, Chief, you can handle him."

Fleck at once said, "Okay."

No structure of such complexity was ever so thoroughly searched. They examined every nook and cranny, closet and cabinet; went over every piece of furniture; probed every artifact and household article; dissected each mattress and counterpane. They took up the rugs and the carpets, they tapped the floors and ceilings and brass paneling, they thumped the walls inch by inch, and they gave the cellar the going over of its cluttered life, including the furnace. They investigated the toilet tanks, the stovepipes, and all the fireplace flues. They mounted ladders to look into the chandeliers. They unscrewed gas mantles. They removed the lining of the refrigerator door. They explored the attics and their moldering contents. They found two safes for which no combination was noted down anywhere, and opened them as if they were boxes of soda crackers; one of them contained a cashbox concealing $187 in small bills and sixty-five cents in coins ("My God!" DeWitt Alistair shouted. "Is this what's left out of what he's been running the house on?"), among other items less negotiable. They measured each room to the last cubic inch, and then they measured the halls for arithmetic discrepancies, of which there were none.

Not that their search was without fruit. Among their more exotic discoveries were some tattered IOUs, well-foxed; a small tole box of baroque pearls, hopelessly flawed; a dented pewter porringer inscribed in dainty flourishes *Beloved Baby, 1827*; bootleg 19th Century editions (British) of *My Secret Life* and the nude drawings of Aubrey Beardsley, both of which looked as if they had gone through the Florentine flood; and three U.S. two-cent pieces in worthless condition and a doughnutlike hunk of stone that Johnny Kripps claimed was a sample of Yap Island money. They found (in the safe containing the cashbox; the other had guarded the aged IOUs and the box of fourth-rate pearls) several booklets of Masonic ritual in code, which produced excitement that died a horrible death when the Inspector decoded them and stated that they were Masonic rituals in code. They also found a moldy velvet bustle, plum-colored; a letter of marque; a chromo photograph of A. Lincoln's letter to Mrs. Bixby; $10,000 worth of Confederate money; and a bottle of bathtub gin with drowned ants in it. But for sheer volume their most rewarding finds were wornout molds for making brass; there were hundreds and hundreds of them. . . . Things like that. Things like that were all they found.

"Well," the Inspector said, "we certainly gave it the old college try. Thanks, men," he said to Giffin, Polonsky, Kripps, Angelo, and Murphy. "Don't be surprised if you hear from me again." And the five old men shook hands all around, even with Chief Fleck, who had got underfoot at every turn, and left looking happy.

"Now what?" said Jessie. With Hendrik Brass's death she had stopped bedeviling Richard about pulling out. Instead, she had followed him around the house during the search as if she were an heir in fact. "What next?"

"The house has to be torn apart." This from DeWitt Alistair. He was stripped quite down to the spiritual buff, mean-eyed, starveling, and ready to bite.

"You mean literally, Alistair?" Dr. Thornton said.

"The old man told Vaughn that the money or whatever it is

is *in* the house. My hunch is it's bricked over or cemented into one of the walls."

"That might be why the tapping didn't produce anything," Keith said in his slow way. "Alistair could have something."

The Inspector scowled. "It's a possibility I've been hoping we wouldn't have to face. But I admit I can't think of anything else. Can anybody?"

But there were complications, all of them entangled in law. The structure itself had been willed to Hugo. More urgently, there were two mortgages on the property, the first held by the Phillipskill Savings and Loan Association, the second by the Hudson Valley Trust Company of Tarrytown. In law, Vaughn pointed out, the mortgagees held priority.

The president of the Phillipskill bank, a jolly-eyed man named Jacobus, and a vice-president of the Tarrytown bank, a sad-eyed one named Claffey, were invited to visit and listen. Their joint conclusion was that the buildings had no marketable value. No one in his right mind could be expected to buy such a sprawling ruin (it was also half eaten away by termites, as the Inspector found a strategic place to point out) for purposes of residence. Various zoning regulations debarred a sale to an institution. As Jacobus put it, the place was a brass elephant.

"When we originally granted the loan," the Phillipskill bank president said, "the house was still worth something, and of course there was the land. The house probably wouldn't pay the cost of tearing it down, which would have to be done eventually anyway because of the value of the acreage, which has gone up considerably."

Mr. Claffey of the Tarrytown bank frowned at what he evidently considered an unbankerish admission on the part of Jacobus. "The question is if the land has a value in excess of the property's indebtedness."

"Let's talk turkey, gentlemen," Richard retorted. "You not only have no objection to the house being wrecked, you'd actually welcome it, isn't that so? Because eventually you'd have to have it done yourselves, and by our doing it now we save you money. Number two, there's been a jump in land values around here in recent years, especially river frontage. Even if the present value of the land mightn't be in excess of the mortgages, which I don't concede, it's bound to become a bonanza, with the demand for housing, the superhighways, and Phillipskill's increasing access to New York for commuters. It strikes me it's worth your while not only to agree to the house being torn down, but also to compensate Mr. Zarbus for it, because it's a cinch the cost of wrecking is going to go up in time, too. What do you say?"

"Mr. Zarbus's consent would certainly be required," Claffey said carefully. "And I think we might see our way clear to paying him a little something for it, eh, Jacobus?"

Jacobus nodded carefully, too. "Would that be agreeable to you, Mr. Zarbus?"

Mr. Zarbus was absent in all but body. He gaped at them. Vaughn said curtly, "I'll handle it for the pinhead," and the bankers looked crestfallen. In the end they closeted themselves with Vaughn and Hugo, and from the sour looks on their faces when they departed the Inspector knew that Vaughn had made a good deal, not so much positively for Hugo as negatively against Claffey and Jacobus. Banking was a pursuit Vaughn seemed to hold in even greater contempt than medicine. In fact, he said so. To the bankers, as they left.

The next problem on the agenda was the wrecking.

"It isn't necessary to raze the house to the ground," the Inspector said. "The whole purpose is to find a hiding place. All inside walls should be stripped to the studs; all flooring should be ripped up, but it can be laid back down afterward for our use till we leave. The old bricks in the fireplaces can be taken out without tearing down the chimneys; and so on. It will leave the house a shell, but at least it'll still be usable on a temporary basis—we can rig up blankets between bedrooms, for instance, for some sort of privacy. Any objections?"

"As long as they don't miss anything," Alistair said.

"We'll see to it they don't."

Several companies were asked to submit estimates; the lowest came from a small one in White Plains in the large person of a gentleman named Trafuzzi. "We got to work on time plus labor," Mr. Trafuzzi told them. "Considering what you folks want, it ain't no ordinary wrecking job. You got to put up $3,000. Might not come to that, but that's what you got to post."

He wandered off while they talked it over.

"Anybody got three grand?" asked Vaughn, ever cooperative. "Come on, you millionaires. Ante up."

The spontaneous silence was eloquent.

"Couldn't we float a bank loan?" Keith asked at last.

"On whose credit?" Vaughn jeered. "Alistair's?"

Alistair murdered him with a glance. Mrs. Alistair's followup cut his corpse into little pieces.

It was agreed that a bank loan was out. The Alistairs had no credit, Lynn said she had no credit, Keith said he had no credit, Cornelia Openshaw said she had but wouldn't lift a finger—the responsibility should be shared, like the legacy it was aimed at; a point so self-evidently fair that Jessie was relieved of the difficulty of having to reply at all, which was also the case with Dr. Thornton.

Vaughn was not a man to let an opportunity for bad works pass. "Why's your lip buttoned, Doc? You leeches have all the dough there is, with what you steal from Uncle, not to mention what you suck from your victims."

Dr. Thornton laughed. It was a short laugh, not expressing merriment; but since it was the only laugh of any kind he had released in weeks, it startled them.

"How much have I charged you, Vaughn?" And he made a secret of his mouth.

The Albert Schweitzer of South Cornwall had been bothering Richard for some time. He seemed troubled, as if he were wrestling with a disagreeable problem. Indeed, the Inspector was surprised that Thornton had remained away from his practice for as long as he had. He had made several calls to his colleagues, each time coming back looking unhappier. It was another piece of the puzzle.

"We have those halves of the thousand dollar bills," Lynn said suddenly.

Vaughn, who since the night of his K.O. had been relatively respectful toward her, winked. "Half a bill is as good as no bill, doll. To the U.S. Treasury it isn't money. Next suggestion?"

"Wait a minute," the Inspector muttered. "Miss O'Neill may have a point. I forgot about the bills."

"But I just told you, dad—"

"I told you to stop dadding me!" the Inspector said, not muttering. "I'd like to see those six halves all together."

"Why?" The Beast of Belsen, instantly.

"Call it a hunch, Mrs. Alistair."

Predictably, the heirs were able to produce their bisected Grover Clevelands on the spot from assorted locations on their anatomies. The Inspector glanced at Jessie, and she handed over the one she had received, looking overjoyed to be rid of it. Her husband dragged over a table and they surrounded it, each clutching his ragged piece of bill. "I'm not going to take them away from you. I just want to make a test. Mind putting 'em on the table?"

Vaughn hung about, craning. "Hey, man," he said to Alistair. "Old Sleuth here knows a con or two his own self. Five gets you ten he palms one."

And indeed Old Sleuth was engaged in a sort of shell game, switching half bills around in this spot and that, but always setting two halves in juxtaposition. In the end there was an awful silence. He had managed to arrange the six halves in such a way that the variously jagged edges of each fitted into a companion half, forming three perfect bills.

"The thought crossed my mind when we didn't find the six halves Brass was supposed to be keeping for you—I mean during the house search," the Inspector said, "but in the turmoil I forgot about it. We don't have—we've never had—the six halves of six different bills. What that old shtunk did was halve three bills and send one to each of six people as *if* they came from six bills. So it cost him not six grand but three. Smart."

"Dishonest," yelped Cornelia.

"He was a dishonest old man," Dr. Thornton said heavily. "Among other things even worse." And he added, with astonishing savagery, "The world is better off without him."

"Anyway, we do have $3,000 among us," Lynn said, "and that's exactly what Mr. Trafuzzi is asking. You know, it's eerie? Almost as though Mr. Brass had foreseen all this."

"I wouldn't put it past him," Keith grunted. "But the question is, do we pool 'em or don't we? I'm for it."

Alistair glanced at Mrs. Alistair; she inclined her head a fraction of an inch, and he promptly said, "So am I." Lynn voted yes. Cornelia, agonized, voted yes, too. And Dr. Thornton looked weary and went along. Jessie, of course, had to play her part.

So they called Mr. Trafuzzi back in.

There was an ancillary consideration. Demolition would leave them facing the great outdoors while it was in progress. None of them seemed to feel that sleeping on the ground wrapped in shredded counterpanes would contribute to a good-neighbor policy. The solution was offered by Richard. According to Vaughn, Brass had specified the house itself as the hiding place of his treasure. That eliminated the coach house, which had five tiny rooms in its upper story unused, from its accumulation of cobwebs, dead insects, and strata of dust, for generations. The Inspector suggested that they clean the rooms, rent some cots, and move in while Mr. Trafuzzi's crew worked on the main building. Lynn and Cornelia, Keith and Dr. Thornton, Vaughn and Hugo, could double up; the other two rooms would serve for the Alistairs and himself and Jessie. The women would have to cook outdoors, but only until they could move back into the shell. The utilities and appliances in the kitchen would still be usable.

A vote was taken in mounting excitement, the resolution was passed without dissent, and they set to work, even the Alistairs. Vaughn kept his private eye on things, nipping regularly at his flask; Hugo hung about with a bewildered look, useless as a child, until out of pity Jessie asked him to help. After that he tagged after her looking happy.

That night there was trouble in the fusty old dining room. The Inspector had been half expecting it; nerves had shown multiplying symptoms of frazzle. Vaughn was regaling the company with accounts of his extracurricular activities with the wives of husbands he had been hired to get the goods on, until Cornelia Openshaw could bear it no longer. "Is it absolutely necessary for you to talk with your mouth full, Mr. Vaughn? You're disgusting!"—to which Vaughn replied through a mouthful, "It isn't what's going into my mouth that's bugging you, Corny, it's what's coming out, right? I bet you take Henry Miller to bed with you. Never met an old babe yet who could keep her mind off her ovaries"—setting off a scene that ended with Jessie's taking a hysterical Miss Openshaw upstairs, while Lynn gave him a generous piece of her mind. After dinner Keith invited Vaughn to come outside and be taught all over again how to treat decent women, Vaughn replying with a hasty grin, "Don't let that fluke punch go to your head, buster. If I didn't have this hole in my back . . ." and the Alistairs got into a wrangle over a pile of toothpicks, exchanging charges of cheating.

So it was a relief when, the next morning, Mr. Trafuzzi and his wreckers arrived and with happy cries set to work tearing the innards out of The House of Brass under a thin red line of quivering eyes, not excluding Chief Fleck's, who had begun to look desperate. As far as Richard could tell, the Phillipskill policeman had done nothing whatever toward solving the murder of Hendrik Brass but hang about, as if waiting for providence to drop a confession into his lap. Brother, he told Fleck silently, with this crew and setup you're going to have a long wait.

That afternoon, on a summons from the Inspector, the West 87th Street Irregulars were back on the job, equipped with an electric drill, a metal detector, picks and shovels, and other equipment he had had them rent in the city. While Trafuzzi's men worked inside, the Irregulars pried out the brickwork of the driveway immediately surrounding the house to examine the foundations. Then they invaded the cellar, broke up the cement of the floor, and dug down for several feet. They used the metal detectors in the cellar and around the foundations. The five men bedded down that night in their cars; early the next morning they were back at it. Wes Polonsky began to show signs of wear and tear; Pete Angelo performed prodigies; the others labored in anger at their infirmities.

But they did the job, and what they found for their pains

were: five Indian arrowheads and a crumbled calumet; an automobile license plate for the year 1915; a whale-blubber try-pot eaten away by rust; the skeleton of a small dog; the boiler of a Stanley Steamer; a metal box full of handmade iron nails fused into an irregular mass; and a whole collection of unrecognizable objects that would not have brought five cents from a pop artist.

And what Mr. Trafuzzi and his men found was nothing but sand plaster and several historic rats' nests, in one of which lay a scrap of time-browned paper that had come, according to its legend, from a copy of *Godey's Lady's Book* of November 1844.

That night, around the cooking fire on what remained of the brick driveway, the only sounds audible came from nature's lesser creations. Her noblest were speechless.

Until Lynn cried in despair, "It's an out-and-out fraud, that's what it is. That old man was pulling our legs. There's no six million dollars. There's no six *hundred* dollars."

"I don't believe it," whimpered Cornelia. "I *don't*."

"Somehow," Keith mumbled, "neither do I. Maybe it's because I don't want to not believe it."

"It's here," DeWitt Alistair said between his large teeth. "It's got to be!"

"I hope," began Dr. Thornton; and stopped there.

Mrs. Alistair glared into the fire as if she meant to challenge it with her bare hands.

As his wife looked anxiously at him, Richard Queen muttered, "Somehow I get the feeling it's here, too. But, damn it all to hell, where?"

They moved back into what was left of the house. There were two days left of Hendrik Brass's time limit of one month.

8

AND WHY AGAIN?

They waited without knowing what they were waiting for. Of course, approaching was the auction, but what could be expected from that? There was almost $7,500 worth of known outstanding indebtedness; time and the publication of the notice required by law would undoubtedly produce more. Still, the place was a magnet, holding them fast. (There was a general tendency to forget about the murder; it seemed irrelevant. Only Chief Fleck's sulky shadow reminded them of it from time to time.)

It certainly held Lynn and Keith fast. But they were held by a magnet far older than Hendrik Brass or his elusive millions. It was this attraction that led to the newest *bizarrerie.*

Dr. Thornton had become progressively more interesting as a study in indecipherable behavior. He had taken to long solitary walks, hands behind back, head bowed, brow furrowed, like a philosopher pondering the perplexities of the universe or a prisoner chafing from confinement. In the one posture he was certainly getting nowhere; in the other he could formulate no plan of escape. In either or both he was unerringly unhappy. Could it be their failure to unearth the secret of Brass's hiding place—his Schweitzerian wish, indeed his need, for the riches that would do so much for so many? The Inspector did not think so. That might be part of it, but it was not the greater part. No, it was something else.

What it was emerged on the evening before the scheduled auction. Richard and Jessie, out for a constitutional, found Dr. Thornton sitting in the woods on a rock, alone as usual, chin on his fist. He had been neglecting himself beyond even his capacity for self-neglect: his sandy-gray hair was creeping down his neck like jungle brush; his red mustache had raggedly overgrown his lips; he needed a shave; and his suit, ever shabby, was disreputable. Also, the adhesive around his eyeglass shaft had come loose; it was barely holding the broken ends together, and he had not bothered to retape it.

"Oh," he said, spying the Queens; and rose, uncertainly.

"Hi," Richard said, and would have passed on; but Jessie said, "Why don't you join us, Doctor? It's such a lovely night for walking, with this moon and all. Unless you'd rather be alone?"

"My God, no," Thornton said; and he fell in step with them. But mutely; Jessie could not even get him to talk about his youthful experiences in Papua, where he had made a pioneer study of yaws—one of his fondest reminiscences. So after a while the Queens abandoned their efforts, and the three trudged in silence toward the Hudson.

They came on Lynn and Keith as the best things—and the worst—are so often come upon, with shocking unexpectedness. The two young people were lying on the ruins of the dock, in the moonlight, passionately embracing. From the stormy music of their breathing and the wild dance of their hands it was all too clear where the pas de deux was tending; and Richard and Jessie jumped back in embarrassment, expecting Dr. Thornton to follow. But to their amazement the amazing doctor uttered a strangled *"No!"* and sprang forward, shouting, "Stop! Please, please! Stop!"

Jessie could have died. Lynn and Keith scrambled to their feet, looking madly around, Lynn smoothing her skirt, Keith making absurd brushing gestures, and both crimson in the moonlight.

"We-were-you-are," stammered Keith.

"We-were-admiring," and that was as far as Lynn could get too. They just stood there on the dock, and in it, condemned.

"I beg your pardon," Dr. Thornton said; he was gasping as if he had asthma. "I beg your pardon must humbly. But you don't know. You can't know. Nothing in the world but one thing would have made me . . ." and he was struck dumb again, as if this venture into words only proved how wise he had been in his taciturity. Then, with a great effort, he said, "This has gone too far. I have gone too far, I mean, to back out now. You'll forgive me when you hear what I have to say. We had better go back to the house. This—believe it or not—involves everybody."

How they got back to the eviscerated cadaver that was now The House of Brass Jessie never clearly remembered. All she could recall afterward was the crunching of five pairs of feet, that of two pairs receding rapidly before them—Lynn running, Keith running after her. Then Jessie found herself in the wreckage of the parlor surrounded by eyes, with Richard gripping her shoulder from behind; and the guilty pair at bay, Lynn still smoothing her skirt, Keith still brushing himself, both unconsciously, and both as angry white as they had been crimson.

"What's the hangup this time?" Vaughn asked, lowering his flask to stare. "The hippies been swinging?"

"You shut your foul mouth," Thornton said to him; and, oddly, Vaughn did. The voyager from South Cornwall turned to the young couple with resolution; he had set his course, and he was not about to trim his sails. "Miss O'Neill—Lynn, if you don't mind my calling you that—and Palmer, Keith, you won't understand at first why I'm going to talk about your most personal feelings publicly this way. But believe me, please, you'll forgive me before I'm through.

"It's given me a hard time," he said, "a very hard time. Watching your relationship grow. Reluctant to interfere. Hoping it wouldn't come to this—"

"What business is it of yours, Doctor?" Keith demanded, tight-lipped. "Or anybody's? Lynn and I haven't made any secret of our interest in each other. You'd think we were committing a crime!"

"You were about to."

"What year are you living in, Doctor?"

"No, no, you don't understand—"

"I still can't believe that a person as decent as you, Doctor, could do what you've done tonight," Lynn said in a very controlled voice. But Jessie saw her hands trembling. "I suppose you're referring to the fact that there's a Mrs. Keith Palmer and a little Palmer named Sam. Well, it so happens I know all about them. He told me."

"I don't know what you're talking about, Lynn," Dr. Thornton said. "If Keith is married and has a child it's news to me."

"It's none of your business!" Keith growled.

"Please, Keith, let me get on with this thing. The fact that you're married and may be contemplating divorce in order to marry Lynn, if that's your intention—"

"That's his intention," Lynn said with a snap. "Yes, Doctor, that's exactly his intention. Isn't it, Keith?"

"Well," Keith said, "yes. Yes, sure. Of course. What else?"

"—doesn't alter what I have to say one bit. Except to make my speech even more necessary. May I go on?"

The Queens saw the young couple exchange glances. They were no longer marooned in anger: now they were at sea.

"All right, Doctor," Keith said; oddly, he seemed to brace himself. Lynn saw it, and it brought the slightest cloud to her sunny face. "Speak your piece."

Thornton began to pace, marshaling his thoughts. The Alistairs looked alarmed, Vaughn alert, Cornelia Openshaw sniffishly eager, as if she had stumbled on a dirty book and was in the act of reading it before complaining to the police.

"I hardly know where to start," Thornton began; but he did know, or he found the answer as he spoke, for he went on abruptly. "We've all been tangled up in a mystery since we got here—three mysteries.

"The first: Why did Brass make six people he didn't know—and had never seen before—his heirs?

"The second: Does the six million dollar fortune exist? And if it does, in what form and where is it?

"And third: Which of us killed him for it?"

The Inspector in his intentness nodded. Thornton was exactly right. Those were the problems. On second thought, it was natural that the doctor should see them so clearly and express them so succinctly. He was a man trained in the observation and analysis of facts.

"I'm not a detective. I can't answer the second and third questions. But unfortunately I can throw light on the first."

Hugo had laid a fire—the spring nights near the river were chilly—and the firelight as usual was playing with the brass. Its twinkling illuminated Thornton's shagginess and made him look larger than life, and somehow menacing.

"For some time I've been trying to decide whether to tell you what I know—what I've known since the night Brass told us his baptismal name was Simon, not Hendrik. Tonight," he said, glancing at Lynn and Keith and away, in despair, "my hand was forced. I simply couldn't allow you two young people to go any further in your romance. Just before my mother died she told me something that had been on her conscience for half a lifetime and that she had kept a secret from everyone, including my father . . . the man I had been brought up to believe was my father. Well, it seemed he was not. And Mother told me the name of the man who was."

Dr. Thornton paused, and they paused with him, groping for the truth.

"And who was that, Doctor?" the Inspector asked, as though he had not already guessed.

"Simon Brass, the man you know as Hendrik Simon Brass." And the doctor went on in a great hurry, as if he were eager for his destination that he might rest, "You see what that means. . . . the only thing that makes sense, that explains why Hendrik Simon Brass gathered six people he had never seen and willed them his estate in equal shares, is that—like me—you five are also the illegitimate children of Simon Brass. And that, I'm terribly, terribly sorry to have to say, must include you, Lynn, and you, Keith. You're closely related by blood. Far too closely. You're half-brother and sister."

His blunt workman's hands, which had been raised in a sort of exorcism, fell exhausted to his sides; and he dropped into the chair in which Chief Fleck was accustomed to diminishing himself.

So the pathology lesson was over. The nature of the disease was known.

Lynn O'Neill did not seem to understand. Jessie read the girl's face as though it were a hospital chart. First she whitened—shock, a total incomprehension. Then her eyes took on the gloss that came over the eyes of all the newly dead Jessie had ever pulled a sheet over. And finally understanding, in a flood; and with it horror, shame, sickness of spirit—the debris of a cataclysm of nature.

The most inhuman cry she had ever heard from a human mouth came to Jessie's stupefied ears. And Lynn ran out, almost toppling Dr. Thornton in her flight.

Keith, like some alarmed house dog, raced after her.

And, to Jessie's astonishment, Richard ran after Keith.

What pigs people are, Jessie thought. Even me.

All through the ensuing babble—Cornelia Openshaw's strident protestations against the very notion that her heavenly father might have been a cuckold; DeWitt Alistair's spitting routine (into the fire just past Dr. Thornton's head), his profane refusal to consider any possibility of his mother's fall from grace (Alistair, who Jessie would have taken her oath possessed the filial allegiance of a Dungeness crab)—throughout the confusion Jessie sat with closed eyes, torn between her suffering for Lynn and her prayers of thankfulness that she was not the Jessie Sherwood fate and Hendrik Brass had decreed. Jessie had strong memories of her parents. Her mother had held Victorian convictions in the sole ownership of wives by their husbands; and her father, if he had ever looked on another woman with lust, would have dropped to his knees before the Baptist God he worshiped throughout the week, up to as well as including Sundays, and risen cleansed.

The protests had run their course and dropped off to mutterings when, unexpectedly, Richard Queen returned with Lynn O'Neill and Keith Palmer in tow. He was herding them like a shepherd; and—it was beyond belief—they seemed exactly as untroubled as sheep. Lynn was alive again. Bewildered, but alive. And more. And Keith looked like the proverbial condemned prisoner immediately following his reprieve. The couple stood to one side, hands entwined, quietly.

And the Inspector strode to the middle of the parlor and said briskly, "Dr. Thornton."

"Sir?" Thornton raised his head.

"That the younger brother, Simon, the one we knew as Hendrik, could have had an affair with every woman his older brother had run afoul of in this case would be just too much of a coincidence to swallow. I don't believe it for a second."

"That's what I've been telling him!" cried Alistair.

"Take your parents, Alistair. Wes Polonsky, who investigated your family for me and found out that the original Hendrik—Hendrik Willem—had been pushed to the wall by your father over a gambling debt, has found out subsequently that the younger one, Simon—our Hendrik—belonged to the old Lawn Tennis Club around the same time that your mother was a member. But there's no evidence they even knew each other. Or, if they did, had more than a nodding acquaintance."

"One man's nod," said Dr. Thornton; and bit his lip, avoiding the two young people whose lives he had sickened and who, miraculously, seemed to have regained their health.

"Granted, Doctor. But I have conclusive evidence in at least one case, thank the Lord. Johnny Kripps did some followup work for me on Simon, and he discovered that throughout that whole time when Hendrik Willem was raising hell out West and getting into that trouble with Sheriff O'Neill—and out of it by a technicality—Simon was here back East. As a matter of fact, there's reason to believe that Simon never in his life even set foot in Wyoming. Miss O'Neill, what did I ask you when I ran after you?"

"Whether my mother ever lived anywhere but in Wyoming," Lynn said dreamily.

"And what was your answer?"

"That she was born there and died there—lived there her entire life."

"So there goes your theory, Doctor, about all of you being Brass's illegitimate children. In your case we have to accept it as true, since your mother told you the story on her deathbed. But I see no basis for believing it about any of the others."

"Then I ask you again," said Dr. Thornton. "If we aren't all Brass's bastards, why did he ask us here? Why did he make us his heirs?"

"Because he *thought* he was the father of all six. In my book, Doctor, the old man was senile. You saw his behavior. He might have been on the borderline—clear about some things, hallucinating about others. And I don't have to tell you about sex delusions in senility. His mind must have been a hodgepodge of memories about his older brother's wild-oats days, and he simply took them over—applied them to himself, and twisted nearly all of them in the process; my men proved that what Hendrik Simon claimed about his older brother was just the opposite in every case. Incidentally, I'm no psychologist, but I'm betting there's a connection between Simon's identifying with his brother's life at the same time that he followed the family tradition and took over the name Hendrik when the real Hendrik died."

"Could be," Thornton said, but he did not sound convinced. "At any rate, Inspector, all you've settled for sure is that, of the six people involved, Lynn is in the clear."

"And me," Alistair snarled.

"Not you, Alistair. As far as I'm concerned, your case has to be listed as doubtful. And by the way, Lynn, I'm overjoyed about what the Inspector's friend found out. It removes any impediment between you and Keith."

"Yes," Lynn said. "Oh, yes."

"Oh, yes?" hissed Cornelia. "And what about his wife and child? No impediment! I've never in all my life heard of people acting so shamelessly. Mr. Palmer, you can be very sure I'm going to tell your wife what's been going on here!"

Mr. Palmer said nothing.

"I'm with you, baby," Vaughn said. He rose, stretched, yawned, made a face, and said, "How about our vittles, chicks? Or is Hugo back in the kitchen? I'm hungry as a wolf."

"It appears that you're not the only wolf around here, Mr. Vaughn," Cornelia snapped, distributing her largesse.

Mercifully, Hugo appeared. From some antique trunk, and for some incredible reason, he had resurrected a butler's outfit, green with age.

"Dinner," said the heir to The House of Brass, *molto vibrato*, "is ready."

Dinner was ready, but it was also inedible and dismal, unbrightened by the dining-room fire and the fat candles sputtering in the great brass sconces on the table. Nobody had an appetite but Vaughn, who ate wolfishly, as predicted. After the coffee (there was no dessert, to Vaughn's uninhibited disgust) they all took refuge in their blanket-hung shells of bedrooms. Plaster dust coated everything. The pinned-together bedding and linen they had contrived for the walls had gaps in them, and Jessie undressed in the dark. Her husband blundered about, kicking things.

"Oh, Richard," Jessie whispered (whispering, too, had become a necessity with the demolition of the walls), "I'm so proud of you."

"Huh?"

"I mean for clearing up that awful situation between Lynn and Keith. That poor baby. To be hit between the eyes by something like that . . . and you coming along to make everything all right again . . . I could hug you. In fact, I'm going to." And Jessie did, after some groping.

He was not displeased. But being Richard Queen, he grumbled, "There's more important things to worry about. . . . Okay," he argued to the darkness, "at least one of 'em's Hendrik Simon's bastard, maybe more. But it's a cinch not all of them. Anyway, he thought they were, which explains why Brass called them here and left them six million dollars we can't find. But those other whys! Not to mention the whats and the wheres. How do we answer *them*?"

"Richard, where are you going?"

"To search the coach house. Should have done it before. Maybe the old pagan was lying to Vaughn when he said his fortune was hidden in the main building."

The Inspector was up half the night searching the coach house, upstairs and down.

He found nothing.

9

AND WHAT AGAIN?

"Name is Keller folks how do," the long-nosed man said, playing with the lodge emblems a-dangle from the chain across his corporation. The Tarrytown auctioneer had been recommended to Vaughn by Chief Fleck. Keller had a look of sleepiness which the Inspector knew was an illusion; he had tangled with auctioneers before. "We'd better wait a while longer not enough hot ones here yet to warm up a hen coop." He chuckled.

No one shared his good humor. Most of the smaller contents of The House of Brass were scattered about the driveway area; for all their flashing in the sun it was a dreary scene cast with dreary people. Their only bright moment had come that morning when the Inspector pointed out that "a certain Harding Boyle" had failed to show up within the thirty days called for by the will, and that therefore a possible seventh heir was automatically eliminated from sharing in Brass's fortune. "What fortune?" Cornelia Openshaw whinnied. So that moment dimmed, too.

There were antique hunters from out of state, chiefly Connecticut, but they were only a handful; and the few local people present seemed drawn more by curiosity than a desire to possess one of the late Hendrik Brass's household treasures. No city newsmen had shown up, and the two reporters from the local gazettes were part-time correspondents, so-much-per-liners. A yawning state trooper had parked on the road. The entire police force of Phillipskill was on hand to see, apparently, that he stayed there.

For the rest, Brass's heirs, the Queens, Mrs. Alistair, Hugo and Vaughn made up one group; Messrs. Fluegle and Channing, representing the creditors, and bankers Jacobus and Claffey, representing the mortgagees, made up another; and conspicuously by himself a weasel-eyed little man with a tipstaff look about him—a process server, the Inspector guessed—whom no one seemed to know. He was studying a carbon copy of the list of auction items Keller had distributed.

"Well, looks like nobody else is coming," Keller said. "We better get going." He stepped briskly up on an improvised podium, was handed a tagged item by his assistant, and held up a piece that had come from the parlor. "Here's item number one on your list folks an old Dutch bench can be used as an elegant end table real antique dating from about 1780 it's covered with brass but you could strip that off and you'll find it's prob'ly painted black underneath and decorated in lots of colors like the authentic ones come who'll start the bidding with fifty dollars fifty do I have fifty—"

A woman's voice said distinctly, "Two dollars."

"The lady is making a funny hahaha who'll bid forty-five anybody forty-five forty-five. . . ."

The auctioneer stopped, pained. All heads had swiveled. A bright red pickup, horn blasting, was charging around the driveway scattering people. It was driven by a big man with a purple face. The man killed his engine, leaped out, and dashed at Keller as if he meant to tear him apart with his formidable hands.

"Hold it, hold it!" he shouted.

There was confusion. Chief Fleck quickly stepped in to diffuse it. After a colloquy the chief introduced the invader to Vaughn as one Mr. Sidney Carton Sloan, a building contractor from Phillipskill.

"Vaughn's the man to talk to, Sid," the chief said. "He's executor of the old loony's estate."

"What's the beef, Mac," Vaughn said.

"Now you just look here, Mr. Vorn," the contractor said. "I just got back from a Caribbean cruise, first thing I hear is Brass's kicked the bucket and they're holding an auction, well, nuts to that! You cancel and terminate this here sale and order all moneys to be turned back so my company can get our fair share of what's owed us—"

"Quit flapping those papers in my puss," Vaughn said. "What are they?"

It turned out that, several years before, Hendrik Brass had called Sloan in for an estimate of the cost of putting in "extra steel beams and columns," Sloan said, "to forestall a possible collapse" of the floors and ceilings of the main building. The contractor had given Brass an estimate of $8,000 "more or less," the old man had approved, and the work had been done.

"The exact figure come to $8,327. He'd gave me an advance of $500—"

"By check?" Richard Queen asked swiftly.

The big man stared at him. "Who are you? No, cash. Ask anybody around here, he always paid cash. When he paid." To this there was a general head-wagging, led by lawyers Fluegle and Channing. "Come the job's done, he hands me another two thousand. So I wait. After a while he gives me another five hundred. After another while he gives me three hundred twenty-seven. 'Leaves a nice round five thousand owing you,' he says to me. 'I like round numbers, don't you?' I tell you he was bats. But I says fine, who's worried, not me, and goes my way. You know that old man never paid me another nickel? He keeps putting me off, complaining the work ain't right, some flooring's still sagging, and et cetera. What could I do? Take him to court? How would it look, me suing a Brass? I figure I'll give him more time, him being a millionaire and all. But now he's dead I want my five thousand. Here's the contract he signed, and his signature on this one showing the work was done. And don't try to tell me you got receipts showing he paid me more than three thousand three twenty-seven, because you can't have, and you do have they're forgeries—"

"Don't start yapping about forged receipts, Mac, till you see one. Let me look through the estate papers."

"I'm going with you," Sloan said doggedly.

Vaughn went into the house, the contractor at his heels. The Inspector followed the contractor. Chief Fleck followed the Inspector. Two people walked over to the road, got into different cars, and drove angrily away.

Brass's cupboard-type desk was still in the parlor, one of the heavier pieces Keller had left where it was for later auction. Vaughn opened a drawer, took out a fat portfolio, and began going through papers.

"Here they are," he said. "Yump. The estimates, the contract, and your receipts for the moo you say he paid. I'd assumed he paid the balance, because this dates back years ago, and his records are a godawful mess."

"Then I want my money," Sloan said.

"It's not that simple, friend."

"Just a minute," the Inspector said. He was rubbernecking over Vaughn's shoulder. "What's that about repairing some chimneys in your original estimate? You didn't mention anything about chimneys, Mr. Sloan."

"Because I never repaired 'em. You'll notice that was a separate estimate. The old man'd had some chimneys blown down during a hurricane, and he'd gone all over creation getting bids to repair 'em. He asked me to bid, too. I gave him a figure, and even though he admitted mine was the lowest bid he'd got, he said I wanted too much. Well it was the cheapest I could do it for, and in the end he decided to have me just put in those extra beams and columns. That should have been my tipoff," the contractor said bitterly. "But that Brass name fooled me. Well, Mr. Vorn, do I get my five grand?"

"There's a long line in front of you," Vaughn said. "You have a valid claim, from these papers, but there are whole squads of other creditors."

"I want my five thousand!" screamed Mr. Sloan, looking like a fried eggplant.

Vaughn shrugged. "Get yourself a lawyer, Mac. Now go cool off with a couple of beers or something, you're holding up the auction."

But Mr. Sloan had held up nothing. When they got back outside they found Auctioneer Keller busily declaiming over the rare qualities of a threadbare early American red rug for which he was suggesting an initial bid of $200. "Dandy example of the period and if you can't use a rug this size why cut it up for scatter rugs haha do I hear one fifty?"

"One dollar fifty cents," said a local.

"One *hundred* fifty—"

"How much did that church bench bring?" the Inspector asked Jessie, sotto.

"Three and a half dollars. Oh, Richard, this junk isn't going to bring *anything*."

"Anybody special doing the buying?"

"That little man there." Jessie indicated the weasel-eyed stranger Richard had mislabeled a process server. "For *peanuts*. It's a shame."

The rug went to the little man. "Sold to Mr. Phil G. Garrett for $23," said Keller, banged his gavel with eyes raised to heaven, and turned to the next item.

The Inspector studied the odd Mr. Phil G. Garrett. He became very thoughtful. Then he began walking restlessly up and down.

More rugs were offered and sold; then a lot consisting of milk glass, from a once extensive servant's table, in wretched condition; then an assortment of old chinaware, mostly chipped—all to the same Mr. Garrett for bids that, according to Mr. Keller, were a disgrace to his honorable calling. Keller was just warming up to the next lot—household ironmongery, from cookie cutters and trivets to rust-eaten flatirons and skillets—when Richard Queen stopped his prowling and, in stopping, contrarily made his move. His hand shot up and caught the autioneer in midharangue.

"Not finished describing the lot," Keller barked, as if the Inspector had committed an antisocial act. "What's it this time for gawsakes?"

"Stop," cried the Inspector. "Stop the auction."

He gathered the heirs in the stripped house, while two more people left and Keller sat down on Hendrik Brass's paterfamilias chair in the driveway and began to wipe his neck with a red handkerchief. Chief Fleck accompanied them, treading on heels and looking dangerous. Vaughn listened for a few minutes, shrugged, and wandered off to replenish his flask which, notwithstanding the early hour, he had already emptied. Hugo hovered in the background, blinking.

"I may have this licked," the Inspector snapped. "One of our three problems, as you put it, Doctor, was: Is there really a fortune and, if so, what and where is it? I think there is a fortune, and I think I know at least what form it's in."

The outcry was as rousing as the Anvil Chorus.

"Wait, wait." He held up his hand as a fascinated Jessie laved him with love. "A few years back old Hendrik called in this contractor Sloan and made a deal for the installation of extra steel beams and columns. The reason Brass gave Sloan was that the floors and walls might collapse."

"So what, Inspector?" Keith Palmer interrupted. "This house must be over two hundred years old. It's a wonder it didn't fall in long ago."

"I don't doubt the work was necessary. In fact, that's why it didn't strike me as queer before, when Trafuzzi wrecked the house and I saw those relatively new beams and columns in the walls and floors. I just assumed the old house had needed strengthening. But Sloan's estimate used the term 'extra beams and columns.' Why *extra*?"

Lynn said, "But Inspector. They're 'extra' to differentiate them from the original beams. What else could it mean?"

"More than necessary," the Inspector said, and paused.

"Don't get you," DeWitt Alistair said, frowning.

"At all!" said his wife.

"Look. Suppose old Brass had installed something in this house that weighed a lot more than the original supports were built to carry?—so much more that it had to have extra shoring to keep the unusual weight from collapsing the building?"

The Inspector paused again, looking like Ellery.

"I don't follow a word of this," Cornelia Openshaw said, fretting her purple-red nails.

"None of us does, I think," Dr. Thornton said.

"We're trying to find a fortune, aren't we? A big one? Maybe so big we haven't been able to see the forest for the trees we've been rooting around in. Like that yarn of Poe's where the letter he was looking for was right under the detective's nose all the time."

"What are you getting at, Inspector?" Mrs. Alistair demanded.

"You assume a fortune of six million dollars, you think in terms of paper money, stock certificates, bonds, jewels—all light stuff. But if the fortune is in something heavy enough to warrant putting in 'extra' steel beams to support it, how about—?"

"Gold!" Keith shouted. "My God, you know he could be right?"

Hugo gaped. But Lynn clapped her hands. "Six million dollars in gold!"

"In gold?" Alistair and his wife said together, hoarsely.

"Gold!" Cornelia screamed.

"Gold," Dr. Thornton muttered.

"Gold?" And that was Chief Fleck, gaping like Hugo.

"Gold," the Inspector nodded. "And what do we know this place is filled with? That even looks like gold?"

And they cried together, Jessie among them, in a great breathy outburst, like the wind that blew Dorothy to Oz, "The b*raaaaaass*!"

They whirled on poor Hugo. The old man had taught him how, and he had made a great deal of the brasswork in the house. Was it brass? Or was it gold?

"You come clean, halfwit," Alistair snarled, making fists. Big as he was, dancing before the Goliath, he looked like David. "It's all gold, this stuff! Isn't it? *Isn't it*?"

Hugo looked indignant. "Brass," he said.

"He's lying!" shrieked Cornelia. "Lying!"

"Brass," Hugo insisted. "Mr. Hendrik said brass."

"Then Mr. Hendrik was the liar! Oh, what's the use of talking to this—this—"

"Keith," Dr. Thornton said. "Do you know anything about precious metals?"

"I took some metallurgy courses once," Keith said, and sprang out of the house, followed by the pale and chattering group. The auctioneer was still sitting in Hendrik Brass's chair; the little man named Garrett and the would-be bidders and onlookers were standing or sitting about on the uncut grass. Keith mowed through them and seized the first brass object he could lay his hands on, which happened to be a serving tray with the familiar symbology of The House of Brass all over its face. Keith hefted it, looked thoughtful, hefted it again, frowned, pulled out the blade of his pocketknife, scratched a trench in the tray, and turned the scratch this way and that to the sun.

Then he said, "Solid brass."

He tossed the tray aside and grabbed an object they had been using as an ashtray, which might have been a communal rice bowl of some slant-eyed family twelve thousand miles away except that it was covered with the same Brassian symbols, and balanced it and scored it and peered at it and balanced it again. . . .

"Solid brass," Keith said.

He picked up an old 19th Century fire bucket and ripped off the plating and gave it the same treatment, while Cornelia whimpered like a dog, the Alistairs bared their teeth, Dr. Thornton and Lynn drooped, Hugo looked vindicated, and the Inspector's lips compressed further, Jessie's heart bleeding for him.

"Solid brass," Keith said; and he attacked object after object over Keller's protests, darting about the area like Jack the Ripper, slashing and hacking and discarding, until the driveway and the grass were strewn with the flayed corpses of Hendrik Brass's possessions, and there were no victims inviolate.

"Brass," Keith said, "all brass, through and through."

"No cigar, Queen," DeWitt Alistair said. "Why the hell don't you retire to some old folks' home?"

At which palpable injustice Jessie tore into him, until Richard stopped her with a mumbled, "Maybe he's right, honey," and there was a silence far heavier than the brass would have been had it been gold, which was not lightened when they heard Vaughn's hated voice jeer, "Well, kiddies, you all through playing?" and he bellowed, "You—the auctioneer cat. Get on with it! We've had our laughs for the day," and he laughed and laughed until Jessie wanted to claw him to death.

They could only stand about as Keller resumed his litany. Mr. Phil G. Garrett continued to outbid the other bidders, although now that so many lots were denuded of their brass skins the bids were even lower. People continued to leave. Some new ones came. Among the departed were the two local reporters.

So the second of Dr. Thornton's three questions remained a mystery, too.

What constituted the fortune?

What form was it in?

If any.

10

WHAT and WHERE?

But Richard Queen said suddenly to the heirs, "I'd like to talk to you people for a minute in private."

"Again?" said Mrs. Alistair, not politely.

"Do you want to find that six million or don't you?"

This was a self-answering argument. They joined him in the parlor. There was trouble with Chief Fleck, but the Inspector said something to him aside that Jessie was sure, from the look on her beloved's face, was mendacious; whatever it was it worked, for Fleck nodded and remained where he was. Vaughn watched them leave with a grin. He seemed to be enjoying himself.

Richard held forth for some time. "It's a trick I feel ought to be tried," he concluded. "Call it a hunch. But even if it fails, I'm not committing you people to anything. Any hitch and I'll take the rap. It won't cost you a cent."

"But darling—" Jessie began; she was looking alarmed.

"Trust me, honey."

They followed him back outside. Five automobiles of honorable lineage had pulled up during their absence; the five Irregulars were standing about.

"What are you doing back here?" the Inspector demanded.

"We caucused," said Al Murphy, "and we decided the old man needed some old-man reinforcements."

"We're here," said Johnny Kripps, "for the duration."

"And we won't take no for an answer," said Hugh Giffin.

"Bless you," said Richard Queen and he went over to the auctioneer, who was chanting, "... and if you don't want these trifle molds and the mesh egg boiler for yourself think what a beautiful gift they'd make for the lodge or church of your choice—" and said loudly, "Hold it, Keller."

A male voice called, "Throw him out. What kind of an auction is this, anyways?"

"What is it now?" Keller snapped.

"Hendrik Brass's heirs have just held a meeting and have authorized me to speak in their behalf. In their name I'm prepared to put in a blanket bid for the entire contents of the house—"

"Wait wait some lots have already been sold I can't legally—"

"All right, we'll except those items. Let's apply my bid to everything still unsold, including the pieces that are still in the house."

"I won't agree to any such deal!" shouted Mr. Fluegle. "My clients have a claim—"

"So have mine," shouted Mr. Channing. "I won't be party to any deal that might jeopardize the full amount of their claims."

"Neither will I!" Fluegle shouted.

"I understand that, gentlemen," the Inspector said. "We intend to protect your claims, also the claim of the contractor, Sloan. Among you people the bills still owing—including Sloan's for five thousand—come to a grand total of around twelve thousand five hundred dollars, a little under, actually. Speaking for the heirs, I bid twelve thousand five hundred dollars for the entire contents of the house less those lots already sold."

"Nothing doing," said the auctioneer with great fluency. "That wouldn't take care of my legal fee."

"We will guarantee your fee, Keller, over and above the twelve five."

"Oh, in that case," said Keller in an altogether *gemütlich* tone. "Would that meet with you gents' approval?" he asked the two lawyers.

Fluegle and Channing conferred hastily. Fluegle said, not shouting, "Our only concern is in getting our clients' bills paid. It has our approval." You bet it has, the Inspector thought; at the rate the auction was going there would not be nearly enough realized to cover the outstanding indebtedness, and this was a guarantee of payment in full.

"Slow down," said Vaughn, strolling over. "As executor of the estate, I have a say in this."

"The hell you have," Richard said. "All that Brass's will specifies is a public auction of his household goods. It doesn't bar the heirs; they're members of the public. If they want to bid in on the whole kit and caboodle, Vaughn, you don't have a damn thing to say about it."

To Jessie's surprise Vaughn immediately said, "Well, now,

popsy, you've got a point," and retired into the background for another visit with his flask. The Inspector shook his head and returned to the wars.

"Okey-doke folks I guess we can wind this up in short order Mr. —what's your name sir?" asked Keller.

"Queen."

"Mr. Queen bids twelve thousand five hundred dollars for the entire contents of this here auction less the items already sold do I hear a higher bid Mr. Garrett I got a feeling you ain't going to let this gorgeous collection of Dutch and early American lots go for a measly—"

Mr. Garrett had been pumping up and down on his neat little toes during Keller's spiel. His eyes were darting about like goldfish.

"Thirteen thousand," he said nervously.

The Inspector was watching him. "Thirteen one," he said.

"Thirteen two!" cried the little stranger.

"Thirteen five," said the Inspector.

"Fourteen!"

"I bid," said Richard Queen, "fifteen thousand dollars."

Jessie was whiter than her husband's mustache. "Richard!" she whispered. "Where on earth would we get—?"

He pressed her hand and kept looking at the little man, who by now was blotting his brows with a handkerchief that was rapidly saturated.

"Fifteen thousand bid do I hear sixteen you're not licked are you Mr. Garrett just have yourself another look-see at that list take your time sir but not too much haha fifteen bid"—Mr. Keller was obviously seeing a commission far in excess of his expectations—"fifteen bid once—"

Garrett was looking about frantically. All of a sudden his panic flushed away. He said in a calm, clear voice, "Sixteen thousand."

"Sixteen bid," Keller cried enthusiastically, "I'll entertain your bid for seventeen Mr. Queen do I hear seventeen—"

"Eighteen thousand dollars," said Mr. Queen.

"Twenty!" barked the little man.

"Twenty-one."

"Twenty-two!"

"Twenty-three," said Mr. Queen.

Garrett hesitated. His eyes sought heaven and earth, and finally came to rest on the Elk's tooth trembling on Keller's watchchain. "Twenty-four thousand dollars," he said.

"Twenty-five thousand dollars," said Richard Queen. The little man's mouth opened. "One minute, Mr. Garrett. Are you intending to make a further bid?"

"Why do you ask?" There was a squeak in his voice, as if some part of his speaking mechanism had run out of oil.

"Because in that case I'd like to ask for a recess so I can consult with my principals."

"No, no, no!" said Mr. Garrett. "I object, Mr. Keller. I have a right—"

"Who's running this auction Mr. Garrett," said the man on the podium, "I am and I'm expected under my license to get the maximum bid I can't favor nobody you got your recess Mr. Queen how long do you want?"

"As long as it takes," said the Inspector; and he nodded to his dazed "principals" and strode ahead toward the house. This time he was followed by not only the heirs and Jessie but Chief Fleck and Vaughn J. Vaughn and, bringing up the rear, the five old bruisers from the five bruised cars. "Oh, I forgot," the Inspector said, halting in the door. "Mr. Garrett, would you come, too?"

Mr. Garrett's little jaw loosened. "Me?"

"Yes, you."

Mr. Garrett came, at a pace that suggested he had just been invited into a Gestapo headquarters. Perhaps the fact that the Irregulars formed a hollow square around him had something to do with it.

Inside the despoiled house, feet echoing on the derugged floors, the echoes died and the Inspector said, "Mr. Garrett, the time has come for the payola question. Are you bidding for yourself, or for somebody else?"

Various faces looked startled; some did not. But the Inspector was not studying physiognomies at the moment. All his attention was on the little man, who stepped on his own shoe and squirmed and bit his lip and finally said, "I don't have to answer that."

"You don't have to," Chief Fleck said unexpectedly, "but I'm the law around her, and the law around here would take it friendly-like if you did."

"Well. All right. I suppose . . . You're acting as an agent, sir," he said to the Inspector. "So am I. Yes."

"That's what I thought," the Inspector said. "But you have an advantage over me, Garrett. You know the people I'm acting for, but I don't know whom *you're* acting for. Who?"

"That," said the little man with instant dignity, "is a question I positively will not answer. It constitutes a confidential relationship. No, sir, I'm not telling you who my client is."

Vaughn lowered his flask. "Now how about getting on with the auction?"

The Inspector said, "I'm not finished."

"With what, with what?" asked Fleck. "What you getting at here, Queen?"

"Come on with me." He did not seem perturbed over Garrett's refusal.

He led the way up to the landing and into what had been Hendrik Brass's bedroom. Nothing remained but the bedstead, which Trafuzzi's crew had screwed back into the flooring when they restored it before their departure, and one empty picture frame which they had screwed back into the wall studs to which it had originally been attached. The family portrait that had occupied the frame had long since joined its brothers and its sisters and its uncles and its aunts in the portable miscellany strewn about Keller's podium outside.

"Well?" demanded the chief, looking around.

"You're looking at two samples of the clue to old Brass's fortune," the Inspector said, "that I'm afraid everybody's overlooked, including me."

"What? Where? The only things I see are the bed and that brass frame on the wall. Don't tell me they're valuable antiques—"

"There's not a valuable antique in the joint," the Inspector said. "If Brass had any decent ones he must have sold them off years ago. The others he spoiled with his brass plating. What's left is junk. Lift that bed up, Chief, and see for yourself."

"What do you mean lift it up?" Fleck scowled. "It's screwed to the floor."

"Then move that frame on the wall."

"It's screwed down, too. What are you giving me?"

"A look at the clue I mentioned. They're both screwed down. Exactly. As all the picture frames were. As all the beds were. Not to mention the brass plating that was permanently nailed to most of the walls. Why would the old man screw down brass beds and brass picture frames and paper his walls with brass?"

"Because he was dipsy-doodle," Vaughn said promptly.

"Sure. But even lunatics have reasons for what they do. What's another reason? What did Brass accomplish by it?"

Nobody answered, not even Jessie, who was cerebrating furiously in the unchallenged competition for her husband's esteem.

"It's another case of the too obvious. What the old man accomplished by it was to make the stuff *immovable*. And why would he do that?"

They chewed the problem as if their teeth had been extracted. Only Keith Palmer digested it. Without removing his arm from about Lynn's waist he said slowly, "So no one could accidentally move them . . . lift them. And the only reason he could have had for that was to conceal their weight."

In the dawn of reason Richard Queen nodded. "Nutty he may have been, but it was a mighty shrewd nuttiness. He figured that if people ever got the notion that his brass wasn't brass, the first thing they'd do is what Keith did—heft it to judge its weight. What did Keith heft? The *loose* stuff. And what did he find? That the loose stuff *was* brass. That was the old man's red herring. Then what was he covering up when he fixed it so other objects of brass were immovable? He was covering up the fact that they weren't brass at all. All the picture frames, all the bedsteads, all those heavy old Victorian bathtubs, all the metal Trafuzzi's men stripped from the walls and tossed into the cellar when they made a shell out of this place—*it's all brassplated gold*. There's your fortune, ladies and gentlemen. Strip the plating off and you'll have Hendrik Brass's six million dollars."

What. And where.

11

WHEREFORE?

They were all for running down to the cellar and retrieving the beautiful hidden weight of the gold-filled wall sheeting that had been dumped there unsuspected; but the Inspector said, "That can wait. This can't," and turned to the little stranger. "And now, Mr. Garrett, will you change your mind about telling us who your client is?"

"First of all you have to understand one thing absolutely and positively," Mr. Garrett said rapidly. "I don't know a thing about any brass-plated gold. I was just hired to bid up on the contents of—"

"You going to tell us or aren't you?"

"But I can't! It's confidential. It's like I'm a priest—"

The Inspector made a disgusted sound.

Big Wes Polonsky said, "See you a minute, Inspector?"

He retired to the hall with his aged quintet of cronies.

"We've been talking this over, Dick," Johnny Kripps said. "I'm pretty sure I remember this guy."

"Me, too," said Hugh Giffin. "And if he's who I think he is, he steers for backroom abortionists and chases ambulances for extra-busy shysters. A real dirty operator who'll do anything for a buck."

"So," Wes Polonsky said, "how about we use a little muscle on this character?"

"Leave me alone with him for three minutes," said Pete Angelo, "and I guarantee he'll sing high C while he goes crawling after another ambulance."

And Al Murphy put in, "I'm putting in for a piece of him, too."

"Wouldn't that be ex-police brutality?" the Inspector said with a grin. "No, boys, I think I'm going to have to make like Ellery. Thanks all the same. Damn it, I wish he were here! Well, he isn't, so here goes."

"But just how you going to do it, Dick?" asked Kripps.

"I told you. Like son, like father. Play God Almighty. Maybe I can make it sound kosher enough to give this Garrett a serious case of religion."

They looked doubtful as they followed him back into the bedroom.

"Well," demanded Chief Fleck, "is it back to the auction, or what?"

"It's or what," the Inspector said. "The fact is, Chief, there just might not be any more auction."

"You on a trip, dad?" Vaughn laughed. "There's got to be an auction. It's in the will."

"Maybe as the executor of said will you'll change your mind when you hear what I have to say to Mr. Phil G. Garrett. Because I'm about to tell this pimple who it was hired him to bid in on the contents of Brass's house, which would include the brass-plated gold nobody suspected."

"How are you going to do that? With mirrors?"

"With deduction."

"With *what?*"

"Listen and learn, Vaughn. In fact, I'm going to do more than deduce who hired Garrett. I'm going to prove who murdered Hendrik Brass, too."

Mr. Garrett was beginning to turn greenish around the earlobes. The others seemed too numbed by this time to look surprised. All but Chief Fleck, each of whose two hundred and forty-five pounds quivered to life.

"You do that, Queen," he said. "By God, you do that!" And he lumbered over to block the doorway, straightening his uniform for his appearance before the world's press.

Richard Queen spoke slowly, sternly, remotely, like the Voice from the Burning Bush. Jessie, who had not taken her eyes off him, heard her stomach gurgle, one of her chronic telltale vexations. It always signaled trouble. Please, dear Lord, she implored, let him be right this time!

He began with the first violence, reminding them that the blow which killed Hendrik Brass had not been the only attack on the old man; there had been a prior one, with the bedroom fireplace poker, which had proved unsuccessful.

"What was the motive behind that first attempt to kill Brass?" the Inspector said. "It couldn't have been for the fortune—at that time the old boy hadn't even made out his will. Remember, he told us then that he had no heirs at law. So if that attack with the poker had been successful, he would have died intestate and his estate would have gone in toto to the State of New York.

"Therefore the attacker's motive couldn't have been gain.

"If the motive for that first try couldn't have been gain, what could it have been? Well, what did we subsequently find out? That at least one of the people Brass was to designate his heirs was his illegitimate child. A bastard who's been abandoned by his father in infancy can't have any tender feelings for him. But he can have feelings of hate—and he can want revenge. So logically hate-revenge was the reason for that poker attempt on the old man's life. The hate, the desire for revenge, were so powerful that the attacker couldn't wait for his father to make out a will and possibly leave him part of the six million. He was out for blood. Nothing else would satisfy him."

"But that would make it Dr. Thornton," cried Cornelia Openshaw. "The doctor knew after he got here that Mr. Brass was his father—he told us so himself! And none of the rest of us knew—"

"That last is an assumption, Miss Openshaw," said the Inspector, "not a fact. Any of you but Lynn O'Neill could also have been Brass's bastard and just pretended not to know it. The very point that Dr. Thornton disclosed his own bastardy to us when all he had to do was keep his mouth shut about it takes him off the hook psychologically. If he hadn't talked we'd never even have suspected a bastardy pattern to the puzzle. Now it doesn't necessarily make it Dr. Thornton. You're *all* possibilities but Lynn."

The doctor applied a handkerchief to his mouth. The cheeks under his stubble had grown pale. But with absolution he regained a little of his color; and he tucked the handkerchief away with a cautious movement.

"Now watch what happens," the Inspector went on, "after

that try that pooped out. Days go by, nights. A week. More. Does the poker lad make a second try at killing Brass? He does not. Why not?"

"I'll answer that one, pops," said Vaughn. "Because Vaughn J. Vaughn 'd showed up packing a .38, hired to protect the old squirrel, that's why."

"And did such a bangup job of it," retorted Richard Queen, "that one night somebody crept up on you, put you out of commission in your sleep, and stepped over you and into the old man's bedroom and buried a knife in his heart. It won't wash, Vaughn. Your coming here made it harder, that's all. And not very much harder at that, because when the killer got good and ready he managed to knock off old Brass as if you weren't here."

Vaughn's sneer wavered and died. His glance at the Inspector was purely malevolent. But beyond a venomous "You're real groovy today, dad, aren't you?" he said no more.

"The point is," the Inspector went on, "that at any time between the first attack and the one that succeeded the killer could have made a second try. But he didn't. There's only one possible answer to why not. After the unsuccessful attempt *he decided to wait.*

"Why?"

"Well, what actually happened? When *did* he act? He killed the old man *after* Brass made out the will. Then that must have been what the killer was waiting for.

"He had changed his mind about killing just for hate-revenge. By holding off until he became an heir under the will, he got not only his revenge but also his cut of the fortune. If it had turned out that he wasn't named in the will, he could always go back to his original plan to kill just for revenge. He'd had second thoughts, you see. Why not kill two birds with one stone? That's how he must have figured. It's the only explanation for his holding off."

And the tempo of the Inspector's baton quickened. "Now a killer who's willing to wait for one reason ought to be willing to wait for another. Whoever pulled this homicide is no underworld enforcer, used to taking life as a business. He's an ordinary citizen churned up by unusual events and critical situations. Ordinary citizens have more fears of punishment than professional killers. Unless they commit a murder in the heat of passion they'll control themselves and look for a less dangerous way out of their problems. Especially where gain is involved. What use is a million dollars if you're caught and sent up for life? In this case the killer had a very good excuse for not taking a chance on committing murder. Hendrik

Brass was seventy-six years old. By his own admission he was a sick man. How much longer could he live? All our man had to do was wait and let nature take its course. Then he'd inherit his million legitimately, with no danger to his freedom to enjoy it.

"But in spite of every normal reason to wait after he was named in the will, this man didn't. He went ahead and murdered a sick old man anyway. Was his hate for his blood-father and/or his need for money so strong that they destroyed every dictate of common sense? Could be. But in my book, which has a lot of pages, there's a likelier explanation."

The Inspector paused deliberately; Ellery had not inherited his sense of timing from his mother. There was nothing to be heard in that room, nothing. Until Richard Queen said suddenly, "Between the time the first murder attempt failed and the time old Hendrik signed his will, the killer did one thing the rest of us weren't able to do: *he solved the mystery of what Hendrik's fortune consisted of and where it was stashed away.*"

He had them hardly daring to draw a breath—hanging on every syllable. The man named Garrett in particular, the Inspector's chief object, was in thrall. Chief Fleck had his fat lips parted; only his breathing was noisy.

"You see where this takes us?" the Inspector said. "The killer's normal inhibition against killing and possibly being punished for it and not getting to enjoy the fruits of his killing was weakened by a new factor: his discovery of the fortune. He must have felt sure, from our actions, that none of the rest of us had solved the secret. But now he was under a lot of internal pressure. The longer he allowed Hendrik to go on living the greater the chance that one or more of us would solve the secret, too. But with Hendrik dead as soon as possible, the killer would be the only one to know where the gold was, and he could then gamble for stakes so high they overbalanced every other consideration: *he could grab off the whole fortune for himself instead of inheriting a mere one-sixth.* All he had to do was to get legal possession of the contents of the house—and the gold in it—without the rest of us knowing why he was doing it—or even, as it's turned out, that he was doing it at all.

"There was only one person," the Inspector went on, conducting his verbal orchestra *accelerando furioso*, "who was willing to pay a ridiculously high price for the contents of a household that to the rest of us was worthless junk. *That was the person who hired Garrett to bid in for him on everything*—up to and past the nonsensical $25,000 mark that I deliberately made Garrett go to. When I pulled my trick you all saw Garrett sneak a look around, then all of a sudden start bidding me up like mad. He might as well have said out loud that he was looking for the nod from the man he was working for—his permission to keep bidding me up till I quit. And he got it, because that's just what he proceeded to do. Do you want better proof than that?

"I've shown that the killer knew the secret of the fortune. And we know now that the man who hired Garrett to bid for broke had to know the secret of the fortune. So the killer and the man behind Garrett have to be one and the same. The man who employed Garrett is the man who murdered Hendrik Brass.

"Now you'll talk," the Inspector said, whirling on Garrett, and every word came out like a clash of cymbals, "unless you want to go up as accessory to murder one. Who hired you, Garrett? Talk, or Chief Fleck books you here and now."

Mr. Phil G. Garrett, ambulance-chaser, procurer for abortionists, and bird of very little brain retreated as far as he could go, which was Hendrik Brass's dusty window, cracking his pale little knuckles as he backed up.

He prepared his lips for speech. When they were in working order he said, "I don't know anything about any murder, I didn't take this job on for a bum rap like that—"

"Who?" thundered the Inspector in tympani tones.

A shaking finger pointed.

"That man there. Mr. Vaughn."

12

WHO'S WHO?

Richard Queen did not expect Vaughn J. Vaughn to cave in like his errand boy Garrett. Notwithstanding his glass jaw, the legal beagle was a tough and cynical customer, knowledgeable in the ways of evidence. With Ellery, the brilliant analytical haymaker in the last round never failed to make his adversary toss in the towel; but Ellery did not usually square off with characters like Vaughn. So Queen *pére* waited for his opponent to get off the floor.

Vaughn's knees barely touched the canvas; he was on his psychological feet in a bound.

"Poop," Vaughn said comfortably. "All poop, pop. That's a wild scene you make out. But where it counts is in a D.A.'s office and the courts. You can scare the pants off this schmo here—all he's good for is to shmear a bellhop to open a bedroom door and then head for the woodwork—but I'm a pro, popsy. You haven't got a wooden leg to stand on."

The Inspector said nothing. He was watching for another opening.

"Try spieling that yarn in White Plains, dad. The D.A.'ll toss you out on your tokus. D.A.s want evidence, not fancy speeches."

He thought he saw one. "Garrett's fingering you is no fancy speech, Vaughn. Do you deny you hired him to bid in on the contents of this house for you?"

"Deny it? Who's denying it? Sure I hired the punk. I never get involved personally if I can help it. But now that you know, so what? There's nothing illegal about it."

"Oh, no?" shrieked Cornelia Openshaw. "What do you call trying to steal six million dollars?"

"I wasn't trying to heist anything, doll. That's what grandpa here said. Let him prove it in court."

In the impasse the puffing figure of Auctioneer Keller appeared. This time he spoke with punctuation. "Lookit *here*. When's this going to break up? I can't keep these folks hanging around forever. Are Mr. Garrett and Mr. Queen going to keep on bidding, or what? I have an auction to finish."

"There's going to be no finishing of this auction," Chief Fleck growled. "Pack up, Keller. I'm calling it off."

"On whose authority?" cried the auctioneer.

"On my authority. There's something come up that in my judgment—and I'm the law around here—calls for further investigation. The auction'll have to wait."

Vaughn sloshed his flask about. "The Surrogate's going to have a little something to say about that."

"You threatening me?" the police chief bellowed.

"Me? Heavens to Betsy. But one of these days, Chief, this mishmash is going to zap you. But good."

"What about my fee?" Keller asked shrilly.

"This whole thing is a mess right now," Fleck grunted. "Put in a nominal bill or something, Keller. Now clear out, will you?"

The auctioneer cleared out, invoking the laws of God and man. Mr. Phil G. Garrett cautiously edged after him. When he saw that no one was paying attention to him the little man darted over the threshold and scuttled downstairs, out of the house, off the Brass grounds, and presumably back to the world of sanity, where a man could chase an ambulance and be reasonably sure of the result.

"Which brings us back to the question," the Inspector said. "Vaughn, you say your action in hiring that little shill to bid in for you is legal. Your law smells. An executor has legal responsibilities to the estate under his trust, one being to see that nobody steals it. That includes himself. You're in big trouble, Vaughn. Miss Openshaw is right—you tried for the six million yourself. Where I was brought up that's called attempted grand larceny."

The private eye became thoughtful. He seemed to be weighing the plating of the Inspector's argument to see if it contained gold.

"Conceding nothing," he said at last, "and just for ducks, you might say, I'll follow along with that as a theoretical proposition. The only thing is, dad, I don't know anything about any gold under the brass. Never did. All I was doing was pulling a Garrett."

"Talk English."

"I hired Garrett at the instructions of somebody who hired me to hire him."

"Come again?"

"Middleman. I was between the little guy and the big guy. Your beef is with the top banana."

The Inspector took hold of himself. "And who is that?"

Vaughn put the flask to his lips.

"Who hired you to hire Garrett?" thundered Chief Fleck.

"Well, I'll tell you," Vaughn said, wiping his lips with the back of his hand, "seeing that charges of larceny are being tossed around. It was old buddy-boy here. Alistair."

So the audience of eyes turned on DeWitt Alistair, whose own mean specimens were turned on Vaughn J. Vaughn with all the amicability of *el toro* facing *la espada* at the moment of truth. His wife's face was simply terrible.

"You dirty name," Alistair shouted. "You lousy rat fink. I should have known better than to believe your promise you'd keep this confidential!"

"Sauve qui put, Mac," Vaughn shrugged. "I take the rap for no cat, especially the likes of you."

"Well." The Inspector was beaming. "We finally seem to be getting somewhere. So you were the one who figured out where the gold is, Alistair, and tried to latch onto it through two intermediaries. Or was it your wife? On second thought, you don't have the mental equipment. It has to be Mrs. Alistair who figured it out. Wasn't it you, Mrs. Alistair?"

Mrs. Alistair's specimens spat at him.

"My advice," said the Inspector kindly, "is for one or both of you to talk, fast. Wouldn't you say, Chief?"

Fleck said, not kindly, "I'd say!"

The four Alistair eyes held a silent conversation during which an issue was resolved. Alistair spoke, not bitterly, not belligerently, but with stuttery feeling, as if he were being held for softening up in the back room of a pre-Miranda station house.

"Liz—my wife—figured it out. Yes. The answer came to her in the middle of one night. She woke me up. I saw right off she'd got hold of something. So we got up and unscrewed one of the picture frames. We agreed it felt heavier than brass ought to be. Gold. It had to be gold."

"So you made a deal with Vaughn who made a deal with Garrett to bid in on the contents of the house for you," said Richard, "and freeze the suckers out. Nice going."

The Alistairs again held their ocular conversation. This time it was Mrs. Alistair who testified, as if she no longer trusted her spouse to cope with the prosecution.

"Suppose we did."

"Then one or both of you knocked off Hendrik Brass."

"You're not sticking us with *that*."

"I proved it, Mrs. Alistair."

"I repeat what Vaughn said. Not in a court of law."

"Maybe. But you're in this up to your four ears."

"We're in nothing! Anyway, it isn't four, it's six."

"I beg your pardon?" said Richard Queen.

"We had a partner. So if you're going to throw accusations of murder around, you'll have to include him in." It was too long a colloquy for Elizebeth Alistair. She stopped, panting.

The Inspector rolled with the punch and came up fighting. "Let me get this straight. You and your hubby wanted to grab off the whole six million, but you took in a partner? Why was that?"

"Because we didn't have the scratch to swing it by ourselves," DeWitt said quickly.

"No? You've led us to believe you hadn't any scratch at all."

"Well, we've got a little something tucked away that we never touch. In case a big one comes along. This looked like the bonanza. We decided to risk it. But it wasn't enough. So we had to take him in to make sure we could outbid everybody else, in case it was a hot auction."

"Take who in?" demanded the Inspector.

"Dr. Thornton."

The exercise in mass optics swung dizzily in the direction of the Albert Schweitzer of South Cornwall. That laborer in the humane vineyards sank onto the late Hendrik Brass's bed with a clash of lamenting springs, like a threnody, averting his face from his mourners.

"You, Doctor?" Lynn O'Neill gasped. *"You* tried to do the rest of us out of our shares? I'll never trust anybody again in my whole life!"

And poor Jessie had to cough and cough to drown out the sludge pump in her stomach.

As for her groom, this time he was down for the count. Dr. Thornton a crooked conniver? It was more than flesh could bear. It shattered the Inspector's trust in his own judgment of men, based on a lifetime of toiling in the laboratory of human copouts.

"Is that true, Doctor?" He still could not believe it.

Dr. Thornton was chewing his mustache like a starving man. When he raised his eyes it made Richard wish he would look elsewhere. "Yes, Inspector," he said in a strangled voice. "I've wanted to do something big for so very long. I mean with the clinic. For $3,000,000 . . . It wasn't for myself, God knows. I mean not for my financial benefit. . . . I know that's no excuse. . . ."

"You figured you being Brass's son you had a right to the whole thing, maybe?" The Inspector was still seeking a saving grace for Thornton, or for himself.

"No. Really it wasn't that. They might all be his children and have as much right . . . for all I knew. . . . I can understand now how a trusted bank teller can work honestly for twenty years and one day walk off with a suitcaseful of other people's money. I'm so sorry. Lynn . . . Keith . . . Miss Openshaw. . . ."

Because he was disappointed in Thornton—or in how he must look in Jessie's eyes—the Inspector grew very angry. "I never came across a bunch like this in all my days on the force! Damn it, half of you doing your damnedest to double-cross the other half—"

"Let's not talk about double-crossing, shall we?" said Elizabeth Alistair with a lightning swipe of her paw. "Who are you to act holier-than-thou?"

Jessie shut her eyes. Here it comes, she thought.

"What? What do you mean?" huffed Richard, rocked back on his heels.

"I mean your nose isn't so clean, either, *Inspector* Queen!"

"It sure as hell isn't," her husband jeered. "You didn't know we knew, did you?"

"Knew *what*?"

"We heard you and your wife talk it over. Twice. Through the bedroom wall."

"Talk over what?" He was growing red; Jessie had already grown white.

"How your wife isn't the real Jessie Sherwood, that's what." Alistair turned to the others. "Didn't know that, did you? She's a phoney. For all I know he is, too. Inspector! This woman has no claim on the estate, Vaughn. You made a mistake when you traced the Jessie Sherwood old Brass meant. I heard her say so. Her father wasn't a doctor, he was a mail carrier."

"He was *not*. He—he worked *in* the post office!" It was the only riposte Jessie could come up with.

"In the words of the immortal Fiorello, when I pull a boner it's a beaut." Vaughn looked revitalized. "Well, well, so you Queens are crooks, too. Why you standing there with your mush open, Chief? Cuff 'em."

It took Richard Queen and the five Irregulars fifteen minutes to convince Chief Fleck that he was indeed a legitimate ex-inspector of the New York police department; and another ten to explain, at least to Fleck's satisfaction, why he had not disclosed Vaughn's error.

"We'd have had to leave, Fleck," the Inspector pleaded. "Try to understand the spot I was in. I was so fascinated by this setup—"

"All *right*," the chief said hotly. "But *nobody's* talked straight. Not to me!" He about-faced. "We through with the true confessions? Or is somebody else holding out on me? This is your last chance, damn it. I find out you're still hiding something, by jing and by jee you'll wish I hadn't! Well?"

Lynn O'Neill and Keith Palmer glanced at each other. And Lynn gave the slightest, fondest nod. Keith turned to the chief. He was pallid around the gills, but otherwise he held himself straight and tall and fully packed, like a he-man should.

And Keith Palmer said bravely, "I'm not Keith Palmer."

And Chief Fleck howled, "You're *not*? Then who in the holy blazes are you?"

"My name is Bill Perlberg," the false Keith Palmer confessed. "Keith is my best friend—we're in business together, the scrap metal business, well, junk, really. Grew up together, served in Vietnam together—"

"I don't care if you were shacking up together! How come you're here pretending to be him?"

"It's kind of complicated," Bill Perlberg said apologetically. "He got this letter from old Brass, see, and he wanted to come, only he couldn't—"

"Why not?"

"Because he has a wife named Joanne and a kid named Schmulie—I mean Sam—and he got back from the war all bollixed up, couldn't work, couldn't find himself, tried to run away, made a mess of his marriage, and Joanne said if he ever left her again she'd leave *him*, taking little Sam with her—"

"He loves her, you see," Lynn said with the confidence of one who has just become privy to top secrets, "and he didn't want to lose her."

"Who asked you to put your two cents in?" the chief snapped. "Okay, Perlberg, so what?"

"So Keith talked me into being his proxy," Bill said out of a rosy face. "Said he'd take care of the business if I'd come here in his place. Made me promise I wouldn't give the ball game away, because he didn't know but that it might cut him out of whatever was being passed out. The letter sounded as if there was a pot of money in the thing, whatever it turned out to be, and Keith could sure use money. He couldn't tell his wife about it, because Joanne's very practical and to her it would have been like him going off on another of his wild-goose chases. Why I let him talk me into this I'll never know. He's probably running the business into the ground."

"I'm not sorry," Lynn said softly, clinging to Bill's hand, "though for a time there I was sort of confused. Keith is married, you see, but Bill isn't."

"Here's my driver's license," said Bill, "and my social security card, and my Diner's Club—"

"Oh, stuff 'em," Chief Fleck said; and he smacked himself in the chin with the heel of his hand and went over to where the wall used to be and leaned heavily against a stud. "What's gonna happen next?"

What happened next began with Miss Openshaw, who had a few well-chosen opening words for men who took females in by pretending to be what they weren't—she was furious with Bill-Keith, and even more so with Lynn, who kept hanging on to his hand—and then got down to gold tacks.

"I for one," proclaimed Miss Openshaw, "want to be shown. I'm through taking anyone's word for *anything* in this dreadful place. You make out a fine-sounding case for the immovable brass being gold, Inspector Queen, and I certainly want to believe it, but why don't we make sure?"

"Sure," said Inspector Queen unsurely. At this point he was not sure of his own name.

"Why don't we tackle those panels stripped off the walls?" Bill suggested. "That's where most of the weight would be. I'll see how much of my metals course I can remember. Besides, I've always wanted a look at that home foundry. Somehow never got around to it." Miss Openshaw was heard to mutter something about "I wonder *why*," as she glared at Lynn. "Where's Hugo?"

Hugo said, "I am here," from the landing. He had been standing there throughout in an invisibility of total quiet.

"How about bringing up a couple of those brass sheets from the cellar, Hugo? To the workshop, where I can test them."

Hugo clumped down the stairs and disappeared. Alistair led the way to the workshop wing with the surefootedness of one who had indeed got around to it.

It was an astonishing place of annealing furnaces, cast-iron molds, dozzles, thermal couples, scales, bins, casting rooms; supplies of copper, zinc, charcoal, rosin, graphite, black lead; a cabinet of acids, chiefly sulfuric (used, Bill said as he roamed about in wonder, in the "pickling" process); sodium and potassium bichromates (for what he called "bright dipping")—it was rather like a Walt Disney conception of Vulcan's forge, dim and blackened and peopled with the ghosts of busy little men.

"I'm surprised the old man was able to teach Hugo how to make brass," Bill said. "It's a process that calls for a lot of precision. Oh, Hugo. Dump 'em right here."

"Be *careful*!" wailed Cornelia.

Bill found a hacksaw and sliced off a piece of brass sheeting and went to work with scales and a file and some nitric acid . . . ringed by eyes, to no sound but breathing.

After a while he cut a piece off the other panel and repeated his tests.

"Bring up the rest of those panels, Hugo."

"But *is* it, Bill?" cried Lynn.

Bill said nothing, eloquently. It became a long hot afternoon of lugging, sawing, testing, the air in the workshop growing heavier with each discarded sample. When the wall panels were all tested, Bill had Hugo bring in the picture frames. Then the brass railing of the staircase. Then pieces cut off the brass beds. And more, and more.

And when he was finished, and there was no brass left to test, Bill wiped his hands thoughtfully on his slacks and said, "There's some alpha-beta stuff here, but it's mostly alpha—about sixty-three percent copper, the rest zinc."

"But how much gold?" asked Elizabeth Alistair voraciously.

"None," said Bill. "Every piece here is solid brass."

"I've got some gold fillings in my teeth," Vaughn laughed. "How much am I offered?"

13

WHEN, WHERE, WHO, WHY

That was a hard time. In view of the brass that turned out to be brass, it was a wonder that the group did not break up and dissolve in various directions, never to meet again, except for Lynn and Bill, who others than Cornelia Openshaw suspected were already in indissoluble union.

What held them fast to the wreckage of Hendrik Brass's domain (aside from Chief Fleck, whose grip was weakening from sheer attrition, and who was seen very little now—how could he hold them much longer?) was the very hopelessness of their quest. They were like the Hebrews to whom Paul wrote, "Faith is the substance of things hoped for, the evidence of things not seen." The gold was hoped for, and it was not seen. Only faith could find it. So they stayed.

The case of the Queens was rather different. Jessie would have gone to hell provided her beloved were by her side, and she would have remained there for as long as he chose to roast, roasting with him. And Richard chose. And it was hell. Vaughn saw to that. And the virulent Openshaw. And the Alistairs. And even Dr. Thornton. Richard chose because he was Richard, *el ingenioso hidalgo*, as stubborn as the man from la Mancha.

"I've got to hear the other shoe drop, Jessie. I've got to."

"Yes, darling."

Since faith was the heirs' buckler, they attacked the house again, or what was left of it. The Irregulars were in the forefront. The cellar was dug up another two feet. The furnace was dismantled into its components, and the components torn to peices. The workshop underwent a particularly drastic reexamination: the annealing ovens were taken apart; everything of metal was subjected to tests to see if it might not be gold plated with copper, or zinc, or iron, or whatever. Nothing was.

There was a moment of exaltation when, after a session of

brooding, Richard brought forth, *"The new steel beams!"* Everyone made for the nearest reinforced wall, and Bill resurrected an ancient acetylene torch from somewhere and fired away at the handiest beam. But it was steel through and through. A prophet is not without honor and so forth and, in The House of Brass, Richard was excoriated for his prophecy. He suffered the injustice, unlike a prophet, without philosophy.

Then they tackled the grounds. The Irregulars labored mightily here, too, although Bill and Dr. Thornton pitched in with shovels, and even DeWitt Alistair deigned to soil his hands. They tore up what remained of the brickwork of the driveway and dug down several feet. They excavated behind the house, and to its sides, and all around the coach house. At the end, they razed the coach house, notwithstanding Richard's solo nighttime search long (it seemed) before. And finally they had to face the unexhilarating fact that Hendrik Brass's gold was simply not in or around his building.

"The only other place it can be," Bill said, "is buried somewhere in the woods back there. He may have given Vaughn a bum steer just for the hell of it."

"But Bill dear," Lynn objected, "you can't dig up the *whole* woods. There's acres and acres of it."

"A metal detector," Bill said; and made certain inquiries, and drove twenty-eight miles for a gizmo rented at his own expense ("I've got to protect Keith's investment," he explained); thereafter he could be seen creeping about the woods with the detector, being crept along with by the heirs, through the daylight hours and twice into the evening. On the second day his detector detected something. Alistair and Dr. Thornton dug fiercely, and they unearthed a rocker plane inscribed "Patented 1864," and even this dubious find (it was all but pulverized, and indeed when Bill tried to grasp it it crumbled into rusty dust under his fingers) caused outcries and an energetic renewal of the search.

Meanwhile, relationships deteriorated, too (in one case, as Richard was to find out, they were corrupted). A typical firelight exchange:

Alistair: What happened to my racing news, damn it?

Cornelia: Don't look at me if your nasty little paper is missing!

Vaughn (*to Alistair*): What happened to your British accent, DeHalfwit?"

Alistair (*to Vaughn*): Bumbler! Shut your mouth! (*Vaughn laughs and takes a swig.*)

Cornelia: Oh, you all make me tired. Especially you Alistairs and old Dr. Kildare over there.

Dr. Thornton (*harassed*): People who throw stones. I think we all know what *your* trouble is, Miss Openshaw.

Cornelia: Oh, you do! The AMA would just love to hear what an ethical member *you* are.

Liz Alistair (*acid*): Old maid.

Cornelia (*alkaline*): Shall we match birth certificates, dear?

And so on, far into the night when the Inspector discovered the corruption. He was finding the brass bed intolerable, and in his insomnia he had taken to getting out of it quietly and prowling. On this night, as he happened to turn the corner of the east ell into the main hall, he heard a door somewhere ahead being opened with thrilling caution. So he froze. The night light was on and he could see well enough. The door that opened was from the bedroom Vaughn J. Vaughn had preempted after Hendrik Brass's death.

Vaughn appeared. All he had on was a pair of jockey shorts.

He tiptoed down the hall. Richard followed, his felt carpet slippers making no more noise than Vaughn's bare feet. Where was the man bound? For a moment the Inspector almost leaped; but Vaughn without a glance passed the door behind which Jessie was sleeping and rounded the corner.

To Richard's stupefaction Vaughn stopped at Cornelia Openshaw's door. Vaughn looked about—Richard snatched his head back—and Old Sleuth heard Young Sleuth rap lightly but definitely on the spinster's door—raprap, raprap-rap, rap raprap; it sounded unbelievably prearranged. Then the sound of the door quietly opening and closing. Then no sound at all.

Richard waited for the scream of rape. What else could Vaughn's goal be? He had already tried it once, and had been balked; his libido was not made to go unexercised for very long.

But there was no scream. There were certain other noises—furtive whispers, an excited chuckle, a gasp or two, and then a cautious settling on the irrepressible bedsprings. After that Richard went away, back to his own room.

But not to bed. He paced to the rhythm of Jessie's breathing.

He should have foreseen it, he told himself. The Miss Prims were easy if you knew how, and if the particular Miss Prim was a biscuit shell over a boiling interior. The approach must have been made out of earshot of the others—Miss Prim would insist on that—and the assignation settled.

At dawn he heard Vaughn coming back. The Inspector watched him from between two of the hung blankets as he passed. The private eye was yawning and scratching his glistening chest.

Sic transit virtus.

But Richard Queen's vigil produced more than a refresher course in human foibles. His pacing had been accompanied by thought, and his thoughts had given birth to a remarkable child.

He was still looking it over like a newly made father when nature offered a fortuitous suggestion.

Jessie came hunting for him in the woods, where he was absently wandering after the metal detector and its prospectors. "Guess what I just heard on Bill's radio!"

Huh?" Richard said.

"There's a storm on the way. A big one. It's supposed to be practically a hurricane. *Richard.*"

"Yes, hon?"

"You didn't hear a word." She repeated the radio warning and he came back to her headlong.

"What do you know about that! Did they say what time it's due to hit?"

"Around midnight."

"That's *fine.*"

"What's fine about it? The house is a shell. If the winds get strong enough—"

"Sure," her husband said in a hand-rubbing tone. "That's it."

"What's it?"

But he did not tell her. It could be another bust, he thought; he had suffered enough in her eyes.

This time he did not rush in. He held back, waiting.

The search party gave up and straggled back to the house before sunset. The sky was glum; the woods were like night; a whining wind was rising; gusts of rain were already slashing the windows; there were faroff rumblings; fireworks began to explode across the black heavens.

They scurried about making shutters fast, locking windows. The women were nervous. Even Vaughn looked uneasy.

"I wouldn't worry too much," Richard said to the assembled company. "The outside walls are still sound, and if worst comes to worst we'll be safe in the cellar. The only thing could happen is the chimneys might come tumbling down, but they won't hurt us in the cellar, and anyway the house is slated for complete demolition one of these days, so what's the difference?

After their makeshift dinner the power failed. As if it had been a signal, the wind died, and an eerie quiet fell.

"It's fixing to be a hurricane, all right," Richard said as Hugo began to distribute candles. "If it gets really bad make for the cellar. Personally, I don't feel like sitting around all evening by candlelight. I'm going to bed. Coming, Jessie?"

A procession of candles made its way to the upper floor. Hugo remained downstairs cleaning up. When he was finished he blew out the lamps and left, too.

"Jessie," Richard said, shaking her.

Jessie awoke with a start. He was holding a lighted candle aloft; shadows were leaping all over the bedroom; the house, Jessie could have sworn, was rocking. There was a steady roaring outside. "What's the matter, Richard? Is the—are we—?"

"Get dressed quick, hon. Put your coat and galoshes on, and something around your head. I've got to wake up the others. I'll meet you in the hall."

"But . . . what time is it?"

"Near midnight. I just got the signal from Johnny."

"Signal—?"

But he was gone.

When Jessie stepped out into the hall she found a rather belligerent gathering, some with candles. They all had coats or slickers on. There was no sign of Richard.

"Where's my husband?" demanded Jessie.

"He's gone to wake up Bill Perlberg," Dr. Thornton said. "What's it about this time, Mrs. Queen?"

"I have no idea. There they are."

Richard and Bill appeared from around the corner. The group immediately surrounded the Inspector.

"Hold it, hold it," he said to their questions. "No time to explain anything. We're going outside."

"In the *storm*?" squealed Cornelia Openshaw.

"In the storm. Put the candles out, please. I don't want any light to show."

Bill and Lynn began to grope their way down the stairs. The doctor hesitated, then followed; the Alistairs' nostrils trembled, but they followed, too.

"This another one of your windups, dad?" Vaughn said.

"The last one, I hope. Get going, will you? Or you'll miss all the fun."

Cornelia slipped her hand under the private eye's arm and said coyly, "I'll go with you, Vaughn—Mr. Vaughn."

"The trouble with you, dad," Vaughn said, "is you've got no follow-through." Nevertheless, he blew out his candle and led Cornelia downstairs. Richard nodded to Jessie. He did not snuff his flame until they were at the front door, where the rest were waiting.

"Everybody hold onto the one in front of him," the Inspector said. "Bend into the wind. I'll go first."

He opened the door; the roar roared in. Making sure that Jessie was hanging securely on to his coattails, he lowered his head and lunged into the storm. They were drenched before they moved three feet.

The whole world seemed to be howling. Through it they could hear the trees groaning in protest. For a moment they ran into a wall of wind that stopped them in their tracks; they had to fight their way forward by main strength. No one had the breath to protest, even if a protest could have been heard. At the head of the stooped-over Conga line Richard clawed his way around the swamp of the dug-up driveway, leading them toward the belt of trees between the house and the road. Faintly, as they reached the partial shelter of the trees, he heard Cornelia somewhere behind him scream in terror.

But it was only the five cars of the Irregulars, drawn up side by side in battle array, facing the house. Because of the slope of terrain here, the hoods of the cars were higher than their rear ends. The winds were prying at them, trying to flip them over backward.

The Irregulars sat in their cars; only Johnny Kripps got out of his. He struggled to the Inspector's ear and shouted something, pointing toward the house; and the Inspector nodded and, bracing himself, went from one to another of his streaming audience, yelling, "Hold onto the cars and face the house! Face the house and watch!" And when they were crouched among the cars, dripping, furious, bewildered, he waved to Kripps, and Kripps crawled back into his car and signaled; and then, like one man, the Irregulars turned their brights on, and the roof of The House of Brass sprang into being as in a magic illusion, wavering through the curtain of rain.

And what they saw in those ten blinding beams was the figure of a man scrambling about on the roof among the mushroom chimneys casting Wagnerian shadows against the heavens in the illumination from below; now leaping, now sliding and slipping on the rain-slick shingles; now maneuvering inch by inch with legs braced; now down on all fours, crawling along the ridgepole like a monstrous spider spinning its web.

For he had rigged up a lifeline running between the bases of two of the chimneys, and he was scuttling along this line exactly like the spider he resembled, in a whipping tangle of rope; flinging a coil around a chimney here, anchoring it there, skittering from chimney to chimney, teetering until the women shrieked, recovering, and pulling and nipping and tightening his web of ropes while the night split apart and the sky fell and the wind tore at his clothes and he triumphed over all of them.

He did not seem aware of the lights that held him impaled. Perhaps he thought they were made by the storm, or he had lost his sense of time and place. He seemed bent to a frantic, insane, almost holy mission: to secure the chimneys so that they might not fall and be strewn in all their parts by the winds of chance to God knew where.

And then they screamed together for his life. He was clinging to a corner of the roof, knotting a rope. The whole corner rose in the wind and broke into a flock of shingles carried instantly away. It almost carried the man with it, as if he too were a shingle. They saw him for one moment standing on nothing at all, his mouth open like Aeolus, hands scratching at the air for purchase; and then he fell.

He fell out of the light into the abyss below. And the rope to which he had been attached came bouncing back into view with a frayed end and danced over the shattered roof and out of sight, as if gleeful at being relieved of its burden.

The five lowered their beams. Along this path of light they all made their way, clawing at the wind, for the place where the man had fallen.

And they came upon him at last around the corner of the building, half buried by the piece of roof that had given way under him, so that only his torso and his head were visible, the head lying at an impossible angle, rain pelting the blood out of his sodden hair and down his grotesque face and into the earth.

"Broke his neck," Dr. Thornton shouted, looking up. "He's dead."

At that moment, by some freak of the storm, or as if it had been waiting for a cue, the wind died, the howling stopped, the rain fell off to a whisper, and Richard Queen said distinctly, "It's just as well. He murdered Hendrik Brass."

It was the butler, Hugo.

Mr. Pealing came out from town and very kindly buried Hugo Zarbus beside his master, giving the lie to the detractors of the mortuary profession, and departed not to be seen at The House of Brass again. Only then did Richard Queen, in spite of the universal demand, led by Chief Fleck, voice the elegy.

"We figured out long ago," the Inspector said, "that old Hendrik had the walls and floors strengthened because he expected to put a strain on them—extra weight they hadn't been built to support. And that the extra weight had to be his fortune—in gold. The question is, Why didn't we find it? Why was the immovable stuff—the wall paneling, the picture frames, the beds, the bathtubs—not brass-plated gold after all, but brass through and through? Why can't we locate gold in any form in the house, where Brass told Vaughn the fortune would be found? Was Brass lying? Or had he been telling the truth—*the truth as he believed it to be*?"

"You mean," cried Bill, "the old man thought the gold was in the house when all the time it wasn't?"

"I mean," replied Richard Queen grimly, "that the old man was fooled, yes. And when I realized that, everything gelled. It's easy enough to fool a blind man about a thing like that if you set out to. Once the permanent work was done and the frames, for instance, were screwed to the walls, how could Hendrik tell they weren't gold? He couldn't make chemical tests. They were immovable, so he couldn't make weight tests. All he could do was touch the things, and touch wouldn't tell him he'd been double-crossed.

"And who could have double-crossed him? Only Hugo Zarbus. Hugo was his only companion in the house. Hugo did all the lifting and carrying. Hugo did all the metals work in the workshop! So it had to be Hugo who disobeyed Hendrik's orders and made everything out of plain brass. And Hendrik never knew the difference."

DeWitt Alistair said something irreverent about the recent dead; but he subsided quickly, following the Inspector's lips as if he were deaf.

"When I saw that," the Inspector said, "I saw that now I had to look, not for Hendrik's hiding place, but for Hugo's.

"Where could Hugo have hidden the gold? Of course, it could have been hidden anywhere—in the woods, in the family burial ground, at the bottom of the Hudson offshore, or for that matter twenty miles away. But then I re-evaluated what our searches had consisted of. Had we really exhausted every possible hiding place of the gold as far as the house was concerned? We definitely had not. We'd searched in the house, under the house, around the house—everywhere but on top of the house, *on the roof*!

"The minute I saw that," the Inspector went on, "I saw the confirmation of it. Remember that estimate of the contractor's for repairing some chimneys that had been blown down during a hurricane? Hendrik told Sloan it was too much and didn't give him the job, even though Sloan had made the lowest possible bid. So it figured that Hendrik hadn't contracted for the job with anybody. But Mrs. Queen and I, when we arrived, saw no evidence of blown-down chimneys. So somebody must have repaired them for free. Hendrik couldn't have done it. Who's left but Hugo? And if Hugo repaired those chimneys, there I was right back to the roof—which we hadn't searched.

"Well, I searched it," the Inspector said, "the same night I figured it out—the night before the hurricane—climbed up there by an extension ladder, and examined those chimneys. Not even my wife knew about it. And here's a sample of what I found."

It was a whitewashed chimney brick. The Inspector pulled on it, and it came apart in his hands; he had obviously split it beforehand. And they saw that the brick had been hollowed out. In the hollow—they crowded round, too thunderstruck to do more than devour it with their eyes—lay an ingot of dull yellowish stuff.

After an eternity someone—it was Lynn O'Neill—whispered, "The gold."

And someone else—it was Mrs. Alistair—whispered, "Say two hundred bricks to a chimney—thirty chimneys—that would make six thousand bricks . . . if each brick contained only two pounds of gold it would work out to twelve thousand pounds. Six *tons*. A million a ton? For God's sake, doesn't anybody *know*?"

"Wait," the Inspector said; like a skein of wild geese, they had wheeled as one toward the door. "The bricks up there won't go away. I'm not finished. I said last night that it was Hugo who killed the old man—"

"Yeah," Chief Fleck said heavily; he was staring at the contents of the broken brick as if he could not see enough of it. The Inspector's violent verb brought him back to his old vision of the press conference and his day in the sun. "If he stole the gold out from under the old man's nose, why did he wait all this time? He could have knocked off Brass years ago—"

"Even Hugo's limited intelligence—although it wasn't half as limited as he led us to believe—realized that if he did that, Chief, he'd be collared for it. With the two of them living alone, who else would be the logical suspect?

"But when Brass gathered these people here Hugo saw the whole thing fall into his lap. They were heirs to the fortune. With the gold safely stashed in the chimneys, and a bunch of made-to-order patsies as suspects, Hugo made his play. He sneaked into Brass's room, attacked him with the brass poker, and left him for dead. He was really shook up afterward—not because one of us had tried to kill the old man, as we assumed, but because *his* try had failed.

"His second try he took no chances. That was the night, you'll recall, when he took one of his few nights off and went to that beer joint. He must have guzzled just enough to make his drunk alibi look good the next morning, sneaked back to the house in the middle of the night, crept up on Vaughn and stabbed him in the back with the brass knife, then yanked the knife out and gone into the old man's bedroom and this time made sure. He deliberately left his Honda in the bushes off the road and got into bed with his clothes on to support his drunk alibi."

"That hunk of lard?" Vaughn said incredulously. "He did all that?"

"You'd better believe it, Vaughn. He pulled the wool over everybody's eyes, including old Brass's blind ones."

"But proof," Fleck said fretfully. "I got to have proof."

"Who else could it have been, Chief? Take that first try of his—the poker attempt that failed. At the time it didn't seem to make sense. We naturally figured one of the heirs had done it. But the try was made before the old man wrote his will. I built up a fancy case about hate-revenge, but I was wrong about the heirs to the six million dollars. The fact remained that at that particular time no potential heir would have attacked the source of at least a million dollars—not with the payoff just around the corner. So that let the heirs out. That meant it was done by somebody who was *not* an heir. And how many of us were not heirs? Me, my wife, Mrs. Alistair, and Bill Perlberg—Vaughn wasn't even here. My wife and I certainly didn't have any reason to try to kill old Brass. Mrs. Alistair would have cut her arm off before she did anything to hurt her husband's chances of inheriting a bonanza. Bill Perlberg? He wasn't personally involved at all, except in protection of Keith Palmer's interests.

"There was nobody left it could have been but Hugo."

"I don't understand something," DeWitt Alistair muttered. "Why did Hugo have to kill the old man? He already had the gold, and Brass had no way of knowing he had it. All Hugo had to do was wait for the old boy to kick off naturally—"

"Hate," the Inspector said. "It has to get back to that, with the heirs eliminated. For years Hugo'd been practically a slave to Hendrik Brass—abused, insulted, worked like a dray horse . . . held in such contempt that what the old man in his malicious way left Hugo in his will was a worthless house and a hopelessly mortgaged piece of land the banks would take away from him the first thing. Our coming here triggered Hugo's hate. He saw his opportunity, and he took it."

"But when you solved the mystery of where Hugo had hidden the gold, Inspector," said Cornelia—even in her joy resentful—"why didn't you tell us right away?"

"Because I was looking for a handle to force Hugo's hand. In my own mind I was satisfied that it was Hugo who'd bricked up the gold in the chinmeys. But all I had was a mental process. Crimes are people, not mental gymnastics. With the near-hurricane coming, I saw a way to make Hugo betray himself. I made a special point of saying to everybody—which included Hugo—that the chimneys might be blown down in the storm. The last thing Hugo wanted was to have his gold scattered to hell and gone, not only because he wanted it intact but because he wanted the secret of its location to stay that way. I knew, if he made a try, it would be after we all were in bed asleep and he thought the coast was clear. I alerted my five friends, and when they spotted him climbing up to the roof with his ropes they flashed me a signal we'd agreed on, and you know the rest."

A long breath was expelled en masse.

"Well," Dr. Thornton said; there was life in his eyes again, even humanity. "Shall we go up to the roof and get our gold, ladies and gentlemen?"

This time there was no silence, but a stampede.

"Wait," the Inspector said again. "Don't you think—as long as we have a sample here—that Bill ought to test it for quality? See what grade it is, and so forth?"

"That's a smart idea," Alistair said hoarsely, running back. "I'll get your testing stuff from the workshop, Bill!" And he ran off.

They waited. Bill was turning the yellowish brick over in the light of the lamps with a peculiar expression. When Alistair came rushing back Bill went to work with the acid and the scales.

And finally he looked up.

"This isn't gold," he said. "It's brass."

"I know it," the Inspector said in the total hush. "I tested it the night I found it. Plus a number of other bricks from other chimneys, picked at random. They're all brass.

"There never was any six million dollars, in gold or any other form," Richard Queen said. "It was all a pipe dream, neighbors. A lunatic's fantasy and a halfwit's dream. Old Hendrik was probably down to a few thousand dollars in currency, and in his dotage he built up this big deal about gold. I'm sure he thought his brass *was* gold. And he sold poor Hugo on it, too—what did Hugo know about gold, or brass, or anything else? So the lunatic fooled the halfwit, and the halfwit double-crossed the lunatic, and they both made monkeys out of you. Hendrik led you down his particular garden path, dangling the brass he thought was gold under your noses and having himself one whale of a time. What that fool's gold did to you individually you can live over in your nightmares."

So it was all answered—the when, the where, the who, and the why.

14

WHO and WHY?

It was the Alistairs who led the diaspora, fleeing before who knew what threats of the Gentiles. By the time Richard and Jessie were packed and stowing their bags in the Mustang, the Alistairs were gone without an echo.

"And good riddance," Cornelia Openshaw said; but not with her usual venom, rather in a sort of reflex, or to keep her oar in. She was standing outside with her alligator suitcase at her feet, powdered and rouged and lipsticked and eye-shadowed and looking altogether like something out of a psychedelic poster. Still, Miss Openshaw had blossomed since the night of her Introduction to Life. She would never be a fullblown rose, but at least she had budded in a pinched way; Jessie had hopes for her, although she couldn't help wondering how long it would last, considering that the man was the kind of man he was.

"Can we give you a lift, Miss Openshaw?" Jessie asked, to the Inspector's consternation.

"Or we could send a taxi for you from Phillipskill," he said, avoiding his beloved's eye, knowing he would hear about this incivility.

"Oh, no, thank you," Cornelia said tenderly. "Mr. Vaughn has very kindly offered to drive me back to Manhattan. Here he comes now."

Vaughn's battered Austin-Healy crept into view. Its chauffeur did not look very kindly. In fact, he was scowling. He jumped out and flung Miss Openshaw's elegant suitcase into his car and vaulted back behind the wheel without even opening the door for her. Through her cosmetic mask Miss

Openshaw clearly colored. She took her seat beside him, however, head high. Jessie had to look away.

"I thought you'd be staying on, Vaughn," Richard said, "to clean things up."

"What's there to clean?" Vaughn snarled. "Whatever has to be settled with the estate—some estate!—I can manage from my pad in town. If I ever get the estate papers back, that is. That square Fleck lifted my whole portfolio—said it was part of his case record, and I'd get it back when he was good and ready. I sure bought a pig in a poke when I took this job on. I won't get a Siberian zloty out of it. You ready, Corny?"

"Yes, dea—Mr. Vaughn."

"Hang on to your falsies." He peeled off in a vicious shower of mud that made the Queens jump back.

"The honeymoon," Richard remarked, "seems to be over."

Dr. Thornton came around and braked to a stop. He had shaved and trimmed his red mustache; there was a busy sparkle in his eye; he looked quite his old self.

"I'll be glad to be getting back," he said, "to the sane world of brawling brats and women who call me in the middle of the night because they've got a few menstrual cramps. That old nightmare."

"Why, Dr. Thornton," Jessie said reprovingly. "He was your father."

"I'd have been better off never knowing it. What the smell of money does to a man! I'm well out of it."

"But Mr. Brass was a sick man."

"Mrs. Queen," said Dr. Thornton, "my life consists of sick men. For real satisfaction give me a healthy one any day. Starting with myself. Well, you're not interested in my psychological problems. Goodbye. And if there's been any ray of sunshine in this business, you two were it. Thanks for everything." And he drove away.

Richard and Jessie were just getting into the Mustang when Lynn O'Neill and Bill Perlberg appeared. Bill was lugging two suitcases, and Lynn was clinging to his arm like a limpet. "And you two?" Richard asked, leaning out. "What are you going to do?"

"First," Bill said, dumping the bags, "I'm going back home and beat hell out of Keith for putting me through this meat grinder. Then I'm carrying this chick off to the nearest padre and making it permanent."

"Bill wanted us to be married by a rabbi," Lynn said, "and I wanted a Mormon, so we've compromised on a Congregational minister."

"She's going to be the first lady Secretary of State," Bill said with a grin.

"And we're going to have four children."

Bill looked startled. "Two and a half is the American average."

"Four," Lynn said firmly. "Two boys and two girls."

"Four boys."

"Darling! I didn't know you had anything against girls."

"Just little ones, not big ones."

They both laughed, and Lynn came around to kiss Jessie, and then back to kiss Richard; and they left the pair in a continuation of the long argument that constitutes marriage in a democratic society. Hendrik Brass and his fictitious $6,000,000 seemed light-years away.

Their last glimpse of The House of Brass was the thicket of brass-bricked chimneys on top of the gambrel roofs.

By prearrangement the Queens and the Irregulars rejoined at the Old River Inn for a snack before heading back to the city.

"May as well clean up the leftovers," the Inspector said over the coffee. "There's no point, boys, in continuing the hunt for the real Jessie Sherwood, whoever she is. There's nothing for her to inherit—whatever's realized out of that pile of trash will go to the creditors. As for the estate itself—the house and grounds—it's just a mess now; they may never straighten it out. Well, that's Vaughn's and the Surrogate's headache, not ours. Only thing I'm sorry about is that I dragged you boys into this."

"Sorry!" Al Murphy exclaimed. "It's been more fun than two barrels of monkeys."

Each grizzled head nodded vigorously.

"I think it's marvelous how you men have pitched in to help Richard," Jessie declared. "It's a shame you can't work together all the time."

"It sure is," Wes Polonsky said wistfully. "I wish there was a way. . . ."

Johnny Kripps said, "Maybe there is. Or there would be if the six million had turned out to be for real. One of the heirs might have slipped Dick and us ten or fifteen grand for our trouble, and then we'd have been able to open an agency."

"Say!" Pete Angelo said. "That's an idea. The Richard Queen Detective Agency, with a staff of five. What do you say, Dick?"

"I say great," Richard said with a grin. "We could set up an office on Madison Avenue—"

"And show these young twerps on Centre Street," chortled Hughie Giffin, "that life begins at sixty-three."

"We've got among the six of us about two hundred years of know-how," Al Murphy nodded. "The more I think of it, the better it sounds."

"Could be, could be," Richard murmured in the general euphoria.

"Two hundred years of experience," Polonsky pointed out with a sigh, "and no dough."

It brought them back to reality. They sat staring into their coffee cups. Jessie could have shed tears. She wanted to gather the six to her bosom and tell them something reassuring, but what could she say? Old Wes was right: business took capital, and all they had was the subsistence pensions on which they lived. They were society's discards, rejected for the jobs they could still do, and without the means to strike out on their own.

"Well," Jessie said briskly, "I don't see why we're sitting here as if we've just come back from a funeral—"

"We have," her husband said grimly; and at that instant the nemesis that had been dogging him throughout the Brass fantasy struck again.

It came in the person of Chief Victor Fleck—puffing, red-in-the-face Fleck who swooped down on them in all his disgruntled flesh as if he meant to arrest them for indecent exposure.

"I got a radio call from my man Lew," he wheezed, dragging a chair over. "He saw you stop at the Inn here. And a good thing, too! I got news for you."

"Yes?" Richard Queen said. His heart was down around his lap somewhere, trying to tell him something. "What's happened, Chief?"

"What's happened," said the chief, "is that I'm all through listening to you, Queen. How you ever got to the rank of inspector in the police department I'll never figure out. You ain't qualified to stand at a school crossing!"

"What have I done now?" The Inspector was pale.

"You're given me another bum steer, that's what! All that hop about how old Brass was bumped off—"

"I proved it to you."

"I ain't going to tell you what you proved to me, Queen!—there's a lady present, even if she is your wife."

"What," Richard repeated, "have I done?"

"I was getting my records on the Brass case together back at my headquarters, trying to work out in my head how I was going to handle this thing with the newspapers, I mean my killer being dead and all and not even any proof except that flapdoodle you pulled on me, which ain't no proof whatsoever, anybody with half a brain could see that. Anyways, I got this file in my hand, there's a lot of it and it's bulky, and a paper falls out of it, and I pick it up and take a gander at it like you do, and by God it's one I never laid eyes on before. Damn it to hell, nobody told me about it. Bob just slipped it in the file. And, brother Queen, you didn't know about it, either, or you'd never have spilled that hogwash."

"What hogwash?" His heart was in the neighborhood of his knees now. Jessie shut her eyes. Then she opened them and felt for his hand under the table. He held onto her like a drowning man.

The Irregulars were deathly quiet.

"Remember when Hugo had his night on the town and got tanked up in the tavern? Well, it so happens my wife's mother got took sick that night, they thought it was a heart attack, and I had to drive the missus out to Long Island, all the way to hell and gone, Patchogue—that's where the old bat lives—and it turns out the damn fool'd et some fried clams for supper that she ain't supposed to ever eat any fried stuff, and it was only a case of acute indigestion, and anyways it was well into the morning before I got back to Phillipskill and found the call-in about old Brass's being murdered. I was too busy to look over the night sheet, and after that I got so snarled up in the case I never got back to it. I wish I had! If I hadn't happened to drop that memo Bob'd slipped into the Brass file I wouldn't know about it yet."

"What memo, Chief? About what?"

But Fleck chose, in his pique, to tell the story by way of Canarsie. "Hugo'd gone to this ginmill, Brookie's Place, and he got beered up quick, which you never know with these big guys, you'd think with all that beef they could drink gallons without showing it, but it goes right to Hugo's pinhead, and anyways Brookie sends him on his way around midnight. Okay. Now comes the beauty part. Around two in the morning back he comes into Brookie's, and he wants more beer. Well, he looks like he's sobered up, so Brookie figures what the hell, a buck's a buck, and starts serving him all over again. It don't take half an hour and he's stinking again. And getting out of hand—pounding on the table with that hamhock of his, cussing at the top of his voice, wanting to fight everybody in the joint—"

"Hugo?" said Jessie.

"You wouldn't figure him for that type, would you, ma'am, and I guess your hubby here," and Chief Fleck favored Richard with a remarkably hostile glance, "he wouldn't *ever*. Well, nobody wants to tackle a gorilla like that, and he's starting in on the furniture, so Brookie puts in a hurry call to headquarters, and my night man radios Bob, who was out on car patrol, and Bob drives over and picks Hugo up and it took Bob and the night man, both of 'em, to get him locked in a cell."

The Inspector moistened his lips. "What time was it when your man booked him?"

Chief Fleck said with the bitter satisfaction of one who has been long put upon, "Two forty-six A.M."

Silence.

"But they let him go after an hour or so, didn't they?" Johnny Kripps asked sharply. "They must have."

"Oh, they let him go, all right," said Chief Fleck, even more sharply. "At seven A.M. o'clock in the morning is when they let him go, friend. And he was still in a fog, Bob tells me. Bob wanted to drive him home, but Hugo insists he's got to get his Honda, which was parked over at Brookie's, so Bob gets him over there, Hugo picks up his machine, and off he wobbles for home. And there's your killer, Inspector Queen—by God, he ain't mine!—locked in my pokey all that night, between two forty-six and seven A.M. And what time did the docs say old Brass'd got it in the heart? Between four and six, wasn't it? So how could Hugo have done it? I ask you!"

They sat there numbly until long after Fleck stamped out of the Inn.

"Darling," Jessie said, squeezing and squeezing his hand. "Darling, it's not the end of the world—"

"It's mighty like it, Jessie," her husband said, "mighty like it." He withdrew his hand gently and pushed back from the table. "I don't know about you chickens," he said to the Irregulars, "but me, I'm heading back to my pipe and my slippers, where I belong. To hell with The House of Brass. I've had it."

And so Richard Queen—as he thought—dropped the case of Hendrik Brass and his ghostly millions and the still unsolved mystery of his demise. Leaving unanswered the two paramount questions he thought he had answered:

Who?

And why?

15

WHO, HOW, and WHY FINALLY

A wise man, Sam Johnson said, is never surprised. But the Inspector had come to question his wisdom, so it was not surprising that he was surprised, and joyfully, at what he found when he unlocked the door of the Queen apartment and followed Jessie through the foyer into the living room. What he found there, and Jessie, too—spread all over the sofa with a glass of sherry in his hand, leafing through a notebook covered with squiggles—was the best surprise of all.

"Hi!" said Ellery.

The Inspector was so surprised he was speechless. Ellery set his glass and notebook down and embraced them both with the ardor of the prodigal son who has no doubts about his reception. Then he held them at arm's length and went over them critically.

"Dad, you look awful. Jessie, you're a vision of bridesmanship. Where in God's name have you two been? I've written, I've cabled, I've phoned twice, without an answering peep. I had to fight not to call the Missing Persons Bureau. What did you do, go on a second honeymoon?"

"Son," Richard said, hanging onto Ellery's hand. "Son. When did you get home?"

"Three days ago. What's wrong?"

"Nothing," Jessie said softly, "now."

"Then something is wrong. Let me take your things, and then you two freshen up and tell me about it. I'll make some coffee."

"Not in my kitchen you won't," Jessie said. "I've already had that out with your father, Ellery. Bachelors never seem to want to give a woman her due."

"I'm a quick study." And Ellery kissed her and with a grin watched her march off, flustered, to the kitchen. "I don't know why you didn't marry that woman years ago, Dad."

"I didn't know her years ago," the Inspector said. "I wish I had."

"Then it's working out?"

"I've never been happier in my life."

"You don't look it."

"That has nothing to do with Jessie. Fact is, I don't know what I'd have done without her. Son, you're just what the doctor ordered. I'm sure glad you're home."

"You sound as if you've had a rough time."

His father made a face. "I wish I'd known you were back, Ellery. "I'd have called you in on it before I made a complete fool of myself."

"In on what, Dad? Let's have it."

But the Inspector waited until Jessie came back with the coffeepot. Only when she sat down beside Ellery on the sofa did he begin to patrol his most sacred precinct and let his son have it in every incredible and harrowing detail.

They were well into the small hours before he concluded. Jessie had supplied details he had forgotten, and between them they had excavated the case for Ellery in depth.

"And that's it?" Ellery said. He was pulling his nose, his invariable aid to cerebration.

"That's it, son. I was positive I had the answer. But with that alibi Fleck dredged up on Hugo, my whole case—gaflooey. Can you see where I went off? Where did I go wrong?"

Ellery answered with a question. He nodded at the answer, asked another question, rejected that answer, probed again, frowned, discarded again, reexamined in a different context, and frowned once more.

"Would you be a love and refuel the pot, Jessie?" he said at last. "I think this is going to take the rest of the night."

It was dawn before Ellery came to the end of his analysis. The Inspector kept shaking his head at his blindness. But he seemed at peace, even eager and that was what mattered to Jessie.

"It adds up, all right," the Inspector muttered. "But what I still don't get is *why*. What in the blue blazes was the motive behind it?"

Ellery smiled lopsidedly. "In Whozis's immortal words, I'm glad you asked that question. Dad, didn't you say the file on the Brass estate—all the estate papers—were commandeered by Chief Fleck?" His father nodded. "Then they must still be in Fleck's possession."

"What's the point, Ellery?"

"I want to look them over. As soon as possible."

"That's too soon," Jessie decided, rising. "Your father hasn't had a decent night's sleep, Ellery, in I don't know how long. And now he hasn't had any at all. Richard, you're going to bed this minute."

"No, hon, no! I couldn't sleep. I feel full of beans. Son." The Inspector was looking years younger. "How about we drive up to Phillipskill right away? Now?"

"Richard," Jessie wailed.

"Honey, I want to! I've got to get this thing off my back. Unless . . . " He took her in his arms. "I'm sorry, Jessie. I forgot all about you. I guess I've still got a lot to learn about married life. You must be out on your feet. We'll put it off till you've had some rest."

"Me? I'm not a bit tired," Jessie said quickly. God in His mercy gave us the gift of lying, she thought, when He gave us the gift of love.

"Why don't you go to bed, while Ellery and I—?"

"Richard Queen, are you trying to get rid of me?"

"That'll be the day!"

"Then we'll all go. Together, like a family should. Oh, dear! I forgot I've inherited a writer for a son. *As* a family should. It's those darn TV commercials."

"Jessie," Ellery said solemnly, "I love you. Go get your face on."

So they piled into Jessie's Mustang, and Ellery drove them back up into Washington Irving country. They crossed the Sleepy Hollow bridge; passed a crooked and crumbling mile-post whose inscription, *Phillipsk . . . 2 mi,* was just legible; passed the Old River Inn and the by-road that led off to The House of Brass; and so on into the village of Phillipskill, which after a hundred-year effort to obliterate three hundred years of American history, seemed on the brink of succeeding . . . stone houses built by the patroons, which had sheltered the patriot warriors of the Revolution, now ravished by pizza parlors, hamburger heavens, Real Kentucky Frankforts stands, Bar-B-Q bars, loan-shark cubbies, real estate offices, saloons-turned-grills—all in a forestry of neon signs; or casually erased by parking lots and stucco false fronts from which was hawked the garbage of the glorious present.

The police station and lockup were housed in a still inviolate early 18th Century building of Dutch brick and fieldstone. As Ellery pulled the Mustang up at a POSITIVELY NO PARKING AT ANY TIME sign, the Inspector said, "There he is now," and Ellery saw a red-faced, overfed man in a blue uniform, wearing a gold-braided cap, just getting out of a police car drawn up before the building. "That's Fleck."

"You give it to him good, Ellery," Jessie said with undeniable vindictiveness. "I'll *never* forgive him for the way he talked to your father!"

Ellery got out of the Mustang. Chief Fleck had stopped to glare at him.

"Didn't you see that No Parking sign, mister? Let me have your driver's license!"

Ellery said, "Yes, sir," and produced it.

"Ellery Queen . . . Ellery *Queen*?" The cigar sagged in the chief's mouth; he had spotted the Inspector and Jessie in the red car. "What the devil you two doing back here?" You just left!"

Richard helped his wife to the sidewalk, grinning. "You know how it is with bad pennies, Chief. This is my son. Just back from Europe, and I've told him all about the Brass case. First thing he said to me was, 'Dad, let's go up to Phillipskill and straighten Chief Fleck out.' "

"Again?" Fleck growled.

"For positively the last time," Ellery smiled. "Chief, I have to talk to you. But first I'd like to see the executor's portfolio with the Brass estate papers in it that I understand you confiscated. Do you mind?"

"Are you the Ellery Queen who . . . ?"

"Well," Ellery said. "I don't know of another."

"Well," Chief Fleck said, taking a grip on his cigar. "Pleased to meet you."

"Thank you."

"Don't see why I can't stretch a point and let you have a look, Mr. Queen. Come on in. Oh, excuse me, Mrs. Queen." And he held the door open for her with the gallantry of a Raleigh. Jessie went past him like a lady, not scratching his eyes out. The Inspector strangled a chuckle. Fleck had not forgiven *him*. He was the last one in.

The chief dug the Brass estate file out of his office safe, which looked as if it had come out of New Haven under the personal eye of Elihu Yale, and Ellery seized the bulging portfolio and sat down at Fleck's desk and with maddening deliberation began to go through it. He went through it one item at a time, rubbing each paper between thumb and forefinger as if to make sure he was not bypassing any. This went on for a good ten minutes, while the portly chief looked increasingly less hopeful and cordial.

"I don't see what you expect to find in those," he grumbled as Ellery tackled a sheaf of papers clipped together. "They're all tax bills."

"Not all," Ellery murmured, yanking a paper deftly out of the sheaf without unclipping it, "not all, Chief. Though I don't doubt that's what you were supposed to think. Did you go through these? I mean really go through them?"

"Sure. Well, I flipped through—"

"As anyone would who wasn't looking for something specific. Here you are, Dad. The motive."

The Inspector and Jessie and Chief Fleck craned over Ellery's shoulders.

The Inspector said with awe, "I'll be damned."

That should have been the end of it; Ellery being Ellery, it was not.

Several days passed, during which Richard's beloved stayed home putting the Jessie Sherwood Queen stamp on the Queen stamping grounds—"I'm one of those rare nurses," she confided to her stepson, "who can't abide living in a disorderly house" (a remark that made him kiss her again for her lovely innocence)—while the Inspector and Ellery were off on mysterious business. Then one morning the Inspector consulted the yellow pages, tracked down a number, and dialed.

"Vaughn Detective Agency," said a too, too familiar voice.

Even though he had initiated the call, the Inspector stiffened. The man sneered even when he answered what might have been a client. "This is Richard Queen."

"Heigh-ho, pops," Vaughn said. "I thought you'd crept back into your hole with that old broad of yours. What's on your so-called mind?"

"Listen, Vaughn," the Inspector snapped, "I don't like you for hash, and I wish to hell I didn't have to call you. But you're still the legal executor of the Brass estate, and I have no choice. Do you want to get in on this, or don't you?"

"In on what?"

"There's something new in the Brass case."

"You're a born loser, pops, you know it?" Vaughn chuckled. "What is it this time? Some more brass in the sky?"

"We found a note Hugo Zarbus left that tells where he hid the fortune. Or rather my son Ellery found it—he just got back from abroad and when I told him the story he headed straight for that paper as if he'd stashed it away himself."

"You're turned on!"

"Okay, Vaughn. Nice talking to you."

"Hold it! I've got to wrap up that estate. Where did you say this genius of yours found the note?"

"I didn't say," the Inspector said dryly. "We're on our way up to Phillipskill to check out Hugo's information. You want to find out you can meet us there—personally, if I never laid eyes on you again I'd live ten years longer."

"Is it in gold?"

"No, it's not in gold. That's what fooled us. Look, I want to get this over with."

"You're still batting zero zero zero," Vaughn laughed. "Okay, pops, I'll be seeing you."

The Austin-Healy was parked in the dried-up mud of the debricked driveway when they pulled in. Vaughn was leaning against the hood smoking a deformed black stogie. He narrow-eyed Ellery as the Queens got out of the Mustang.

"So you're Elmer," he said.

"Ellery," Ellery said.

They looked each other over like two dogs.

"You don't look like such-a-much," Vaughn said at last.

"You do," Ellery said pleasantly. "You positively glister."

"I what?" Vaughn stared. "Say, are you for real?"

"Try me," Ellery said, waited, was not challenged, and stepped into Hendrik Brass's house. The Inspector, grinning, followed on his heels. Vaughn frowned, tossed his stogie away, and hurried after them.

Ellery was standing in the foyer, looking around at the ruins.

"I want to see that note of Hugo's," Vaughn said.

"Why?" Ellery said.

"Why? Because it's probably a phoney."

"If it is, we'll soon find out. Either there's a brass box where the note says it is, or there isn't. Right now it's the box that counts, not the note."

"It's in a box?" Vaughn muttered. "That must mean treasury notes, securities, maybe jewelry!" He rubbed his hands. "That's more like it. Let's go, Elmer. Where is it?"

The Queens started upstairs, crowded by Vaughn.

"In Hugo's room," the Inspector said.

"What kind of crud you handing me? Why, Hugo's room was searched a skillion times, along with the rest of this crummy pad!"

The Inspector shrugged without turning around. "That's where the note says it is."

"Then it is a phoney," Vaughn said as they reached the landing and the Inspector turned left, leading the way. "It can't be in the ape's room.

"Yes, it can," Ellery said.

"How? Where does the note say it is?"

"In his mattress," the Inspector said.

"Oh, come *on,* pops. You searched that mattress yourself."

"I know I did," the Inspector said unhappily. "So did a lot of others, Vaughn, including you." He had paused in the doorway to Hugo's bedroom, a tiny box of a place, high in the house, under the eaves. It was hot and full of bugs streaming in through the open window and denuded of everything but the screwed down brass bed with its lumpy old torn-up mattress, and a huge built-in wardrobe closet of fumed oak that covered half a wall, its doors slightly ajar and groaning a little in the breeze coming fitfully through the window. Beyond they could see the Hudson and smell its swampy tang. "But my son here has an explanation."

"The search went from room to room, as I understand it," Ellery said. "It was broken up by meals, sleeping periods, and other interruptions. All Hugo had to do was keep one step ahead of you, Vaughn. When he knew you were all heading for his room, he took the box out of the mattress and hid it somewhere else, probably in a room you had just searched. When you were through searching his room he took the first opportunity to retrieve the box and put it back in his mattress. During a second search, or a third, or a tenth, he simply repeated the dodge. I'm amazed none of you thought of it."

Vaughn's mouth was open. The Inspector was shaking his head.

"Well, what are we waiting for?" Vaughn cried.

But Ellery gripped his arm. Vaughn looked down, surprised. "I think," Ellery said, "we'd best let my father do it."

The Inspector's footsteps crunched across the plaster dust on the chestnut floor. The old random boards, which had been loosely replaced by Trafuzzi's house wreckers, gave under his weight here and there, making the journey hazardous. But he paid no attention; he was intent on the bed and its ripped mattress; and so were the two onlookers in the doorway.

Richard Queen stooped and felt all over the mattress.

Suddenly his hands stopped.

"By God," he said; and plunged them into the mattress's vitals and, with effort, brought them out, dragging a sizable flat brass box. He set it down on the bed and stared at it as if he could not believe his eyes. Ellery ran over and examined it quickly. It was chased all over with the familiar scrollwork of the House of Brass, and it was locked with a brass lock.

"This lock shouldn't give us any trouble," Ellery said. "Is there a tool somewhere we can use as a pry?"

"Don't bother, Elmer," said Vaughn; and the Queens swung about to find Vaughn with a .38 revolver in his hand which was pointed at the Inspector's belly. The man's face was a cartoon in voracity and brute triumph. "Get over near the window. *Move*."

Father and son communicated with each other in silence and, as one, obeyed. Vaughn went over to the bed, treading carefully, not taking his eyes from them. He had some trouble picking up the box with one hand. But he managed it, and tucked it under his arm, and laughed.

"With all this weight it's got to be mostly jewelry," he said. "Maybe I'll be lucky and find some cash, too. With ice you always take a beating from the fence. Six million bucks' worth! Don't you wish you could live long enough to see it?"

Ellery said, "You're going to kill us?"

"Sorry, pal."

"Hold the execution," Ellery said. "As long as we won't be around to testify against you, Vaughn, you haven't anything to lose. You murdered Hendrik Brass, didn't you?"

Vaughn laughed again. "I knocked the old bastard off, sure. Why not? Fourteen-plus percent of six million is still a lot of bread. Only now, Elmer, thanks to you, I get to keep the whole *shtik*. My big problem is how to get rid of the corpuses. Probably sink you both in the Hudson."

"You have a bigger problem than that," Ellery said in a conversational tone. "I think, Chief, you and your man can come out now."

Vaughn spun. The doors of the wardrobe closet had been flung wide, and from the closet stepped Chief Fleck and his man Lew with Police Positives leveled.

"Drop the gun, Vaughn," Fleck said; and as he said it Vaughn's forefinger jerked on the trigger of his .38 and three shots deafened the Queens. Vaughn's bullet clipped a chunk of oak out of the top panel of the closet; Fleck's and Lew's tore two holes in Vaughn's heart. He flipped over backward like a trained dog, struck the far wall, and thudded to the floor to lie there in crumpled isolation, half on his back, wounds spurting. After a while they stopped spurting and began to ooze. And some time after that the oozing stopped, too.

Lew came over in the ear-splitting silence, pursed his lips, widened his cross eyes, and dropped Hugo's mattress over the body.

Ellery picked up the brass box. It had been flung clear of the blood.

"You heard his confession, Chief?" the Inspector said.

"Every word." Fleck wiped his streaming face. "You know, I never fired this gun at anybody before? It's a funny feeling. . . . Lew took it down word for word. . . . Vaughn." The chief stared down at the mattress and shook his head; he seemed shaken to the giblets. He's not thinking of the reporters now, the Inspector thought, but give him time, give him time.

"I agreed with Dad's reasoning up to a point," Ellery said. "He was right in deducing that the first attempt on Brass's life—the unsuccessful one, with the poker—since it occurred before Brass made out his will, must have been made by a non-heir, which could only mean Hugo; and for the reason Dad gave—sheer hate. Where you went off, Dad, was in assuming that, because Hugo attacked Brass the first time, he must also have attacked him the second time. Hugo didn't kill Brass, as you found out when Chief Fleck came up with Hugo's alibi. Since Hugo couldn't have made that second, successful attempt, who could have?"

They were gathered in a private dining room at the Old River Inn—the three Queens, the five Irregulars, and Chief Fleck and his man Lew, who was taking notes and whose surname they never learned. They were guests of Fleck, who had of course recovered from the shock of the shooting and was preparing for the press conference he had already scheduled for the following morning.

"But how did you know it was Vaughn, Mr. Queen?" the chief asked anxiously. "Lew, be sure and get this down."

"With Hugo eliminated as the stabber of Brass," Ellery said, "the whole picture changes. Here's how it must have gone: Hugo takes a night off, goes to the tavern, pretends to get loaded on beer, and is kicked out around midnight. He immediately goes home on his Honda to try to kill Brass—his second try. This time he has to contend with Vaughn, who's sleeping on a cot before the old man's door. Vaughn proves no problem. Hugo used the brass letterknife from the desk downstairs to stab the sleeping beauty in the back. But he *didn't* go into the old man's bedroom and stab him, too—we know he didn't, because Brass was murdered between four and six A.M., and during those two hours, and for a considerable period before and after, Hugo was locked up in one of Chief Fleck's cells. So obviously, after stabbing Vaughn, Hugo must have got cold feet, lost his nerve; and he went back to the tavern and this time got really loaded, to land in jail.

"That leaves Vaughn alone outside Brass's bedroom with the knife in his back.

"Now a knife in the back," Ellery said, "sounds like a serious, quite incapacitating wound, and ninety-nine times out of a hundred it is. But was it in Vaughn's case? No. When Dad found him in the morning he was a very lively casualty. He was conscious. He was able to sit up in short order. In fact, he was on his feet and was his old self in a wonderfully short time. In other words, his wound was superficial.

"Which makes it possible for Vaughn to have come to

around, say, four A.M. and crawl off his cot. What would he do? Realizing he had been attacked, which could only have been to get Brass's bodyguard out of the way, he would naturally go into the bedroom to see if the old man had been attacked, too. But no, old Brass was asleep, untouched, quite alive. And in a flash Vaughn saw that, through sheer luck, he had been handed a perfect setup for murder. From the position of the stab wound in his own back, it could not possibly have been self-inflicted. If he killed old Brass with the same knife and then went back to his cot and pretended to pass out, who would connect him with the old man's murder? Dad and Fleck would have to think that Vaughn and Brass had been attacked by a third person.

"So that's just what Vaughn did, and that's just what you thought, Dad, when you found him out in the hall in the morning, and Brass in the bedroom with the knife in his heart."

"But why?" Johnny Kripps demanded. "Why kill the old man at all, Ellery? That's what I can't dope. What did Vaughn hope to get out of it?"

"Obviously, Johnny, he must have hoped to get a great deal out of it," Ellery said. "And the only thing of value connected with Hendrik Brass was the six million dollars he kept dangling in front of his heirs' noses. So *Vaughn must have had a legitimate claim on that fortune*. That's what sent me looking for documentary evidence in the estate records. And when I found the evidence—a notarized statement by one Harding Boyle that he was the Harding Boyle named in Brass's will as one of the heirs, with the claim certified by Vaughn J. Vaughn as executor of the estate—I had the indisputable confirmation of Vaughn's stake in the crime and his guilt."

"Boyle," Chief Fleck mumbled. "The heir that never showed up. . . . You mean, Mr. Queen, Vaughn had some kind of a hold on this Boyle?"

"It seemed likelier to me, Chief," Ellery said gently, "that Vaughn *was* Boyle, as Dad's confirmed in the last few days by digging into Vaughn's past."

"Hugh Giffin here did the actual digging," the Inspector said. "Tell 'em, Hughie."

"Harding Boyle—they used to call him 'Hard' Boyle—was Vaughn's real handle," Giffin said. "He was a Chicago slum kid who got into all kinds of trouble—did time on A.D.W. raps, mugging, stuff like that; the law degree he claimed to have, by the way, was a lot of hooey, because the only law he knew was what he picked up in the Joliet library during a stretch there—and took the name Vaughn to shake his past. He'd never got a detective agency license otherwise."

"Let me get this straight now," Phillipskill's police chief said. "He was one of Brass's bastards, too, right? Hated the old man's guts, right?"

"I'm sure he did," Ellery said, "although in Vaughn's kind of rat race revenge would run a poor second to six million dollars as a payoff."

"Put that down, Lew!"

"If Vaughn was Boyle," Al Murphy objected, "how come he didn't identify himself as Boyle? Hell, he was actually named in the will. Why didn't he do it all open and above-board?"

"As Boyle, there was a warrant out for his arrest in Illinois," the Inspector said. "He played it safe, Al. He hid under the Vaughn alias while the six million was being hunted for. If it was never found, he hadn't broken his cover. If it was, he could take it from there. Remember, he protected himself by stashing that sworn statement among the estate papers, certifying—as Vaughn the executor—that he, Boyle, had presented himself and been duly identified as a legal heir."

"And that's another thing," Pete Angelo said. "Why be dumb and leave that paper in the portfolio? Granted he hid it among some bills, where he figured it wouldn't be found easy. But why do it at all? You say protection. That was damn dangerous protection."

"As it turned out," Ellery said, "it most certainly was. But he had to cover himself, Pete, if the fortune was ever found. It was a risk he simply had to take. Remember, he couldn't know that Chief Fleck would take the portfolio away from him. That was a smart move, Chief."

Fleck beamed. "I figured it might be." His man Lew looked at him, then bent back to his notes. Fleck coughed and downed the rest of the New York State champagne in his glass.

"There's still one thing I don't understand." Jessie said apologetically. "All right, Vaughn was Harding Boyle, one of the heirs. How on earth did he also turn out to be the 'lawyer'-bodyguard-executor that Mr. Brass hired? Wasn't that a whopping coincidence, Ellery?"

"It wasn't a coincidence at all, dear heart," Ellery said. "Brass didn't seek Vaughn out—it was the other way round. Vaughn either knew or learned that Brass was his hit-and-run father, did some research on him—the newspaper morgues are full of yarns about the Brasses—and made a deliberate play for the job. It wasn't hard for him to weasel his way into the old man's confidence, with his private detective agency credentials, his fake legal background, his fast talk, and his willingness to work for Brass at a low fee.

"He could be sure of at least a seventh of the six million—he really believed there was six million dollars in the pot; that old dingleberry took Vaughn in as well as the rest of you—but I don't doubt he kept his eye peeled for a chance to find the whole bundle and somehow manage to keep it all for himself. In fact, that's what I counted on when I set up the trap. There was no note from Hugo, of course, and no fortune, but I figured that Vaughn, who'd killed for it, would snap at any bait that might land him the prize he'd given up for lost; and that's how it worked out, with Chief Fleck's cooperation. Well, Chief, I think you've got all you need. Thanks for the dinner. We'll be heading back to town."

But it was Chief Fleck and Lew who left first, Fleck's belly jiggling as he hurried out, blue sleeve unconsciously wiping the visor of his cap as if getting it spit-and-polished for his consummate appointment with the gentlemen of the press.

"Oh, Dad, one thing before we go." Ellery reached under the table and with considerable difficulty brought forth the brass box he and the Inspector had planted in Hugo Zarbus's mattress to tempt the heart and force the hand of Vaughn J. Vaughn. "To be placed," Ellery said with a grin, "among your souvenirs."

The Inspector looked down at it without happiness.

"What did you and Ellery put in it, Richard?" Jessie asked hastily.

The lock had been removed, and Richard smiled suddenly and raised the lid.

Glowing up at Jessie was a treasure of recently polished metal—bolts; nuts; pipe fittings; ashtrays; some bullet molds; a time-pitted pestle; three wick trimmers; seven trays of broken jewelers' scales (where was the eighth?); several bent-out-of-shape hose nozzles; a beaten wall-plaque portrait in relief of John C. Calhoun; a scattering of paper clips; a guttering trowel circa 1850 and a five-inch Trylon-and-Perisphere circa 1939; a Union Army bugle with the bell hacked off; a collection of drawer pulls, various; and one snapped-off spring of a mousetrap.

And all of brass.